Wrong Side of the Law

Doug Smith

to Hasco Library
Doug Smith
6-30-05

PublishAmerica
Baltimore

First printing

ISBN: 1-4137-6141-0
PUBLISHED BY PUBLISHAMERICA, LLLP
www.publishamerica.com
Baltimore

Printed in the United States of America

Dedicated to my wife Virginia and my children, Terry Ann, Susan, Mark, Tim, and Llin.

Special acknowledgment to the Medford senior writing group for their critique and support in writing this book. Also to Lori Davis for assistance in editing.

CHAPTER 1—TOM

His buckskin gelding was running through the sagebrush and Tom was swinging a large loop of his lariat over his head. He was about to drop that loop over a maverick steer when a shot rang out and down his horse went, with the cowboy flying over his head.

As he was picking himself up off the ground there was another shot, and the dust flew just in front of his head. Someone was shooting from the top of that juniper-covered hill. He dove into a gully beside him for protection. His rifle was under his dead horse and there was no way to retrieve it. All he had was his forty-five. Whoever fired that shot wanted him dead. All he could do was lie there quietly. *If I stay here long enough the shooter might come down to finish the job. I have no choice but to lie here patiently. Might even have to stay here till dark.* The wait was terrible, and he was mighty thirsty. *I don't know who fired that shot or why, unless he thought I was someone else. Only thing I can think of maybe it was the boyfriend of that girl I was dancing with at the barn dance there at the Jordan River ranch. She was flirting with me and dancin' mighty close. One young cowboy was watchin' us and actin' a little jealous.*

I should have killed that half-breed back there at the dance instead of ridin' way out here to do the job. I don't see him so I reckon he's hidin' in that gully. I may have wounded him. Should have waited till he had a rope on that steer an' then I would have had a standin' target. I'm riding down there and finishing the job. As hot as it is he's bound to get thirsty and go to his horse for his water bag. He might just wait till dark. I don't intend on him getting away, the man on the hill thought.

Peering over the gully and through the sagebrush, Tom could see a man riding down off the juniper-covered hill towards him. *As soon as that man gets within pistol range, I'm going to see what his intentions are. My guess is he's the shooter.*

The cowboy rode up to the dead horse and dismounted, and at that time Tom stood up and said, "Here I am, ambusher!" They both drew at the same time and one man went down, shot through the heart.

Tom walked over to get a good gander at the man that was hell bent on killin' him. He was about five feet eight, clean-shaven except for a handlebar moustache. He wore high boots that came nearly to his knees. *Can't say I know who he is, but he was sure hankerin' to see me dead. Since I've been workin' for the Bar-0-1 spread, cattle have been comin' up missing. Don't believe he was shooting at me just because of the girl. Part maybe, but I reckon I might have been getting close to findin' out who the rustlers are. Why would he ride way out here when he could have killed me as I left the dance? I can't leave his body out here for the vultures an' wolves to gnaw on so I best take his body into town. He might have someone there that would want to give him a proper burial.*

Tom loaded the man behind the saddle, himself riding in the saddle, and headed for Silver City. Since it was early June there was plenty of snow left in the juniper-covered mountains. He was riding at a lower elevation with just a scattering of snow. Wildflowers and buttercups were poking through the ground. He didn't have far to go, maybe ten miles or so, through sagebrush and junipers along the way. The town was nestled among the mountains and only one main street, except for a few short side streets. As he rode through the dusty streets, townspeople were mighty curious lookin' as to what he was carryin'. He rode up in front of the sheriff's office, dismounted and went in. The man sitting behind the desk was a lean, hard-looking man sporting a handlebar mustache and a star on his chest. A fancy dresser wearing jeans, shiny boots, a black vest with silver buttons and the look of a man not to trifle with.

"Are you the sheriff?"

"I reckon this star on my chest answers that question! What do you want, cowboy?"

"I have a man behind my saddle that tried to bushwhack me a few miles south of here."

The sheriff swung his feet off his desk and stood up. He was a big man, must have been at least six feet four and not an ounce of fat on him. "Let's go take a look at him, cowboy," he said, as he put on his Stetson.

Tom walked out with the sheriff behind him. The sheriff raised the head of the dead cowboy to get a look at his face. "Why, this is young Charlie Benson! He sometimes could be a little hotheaded, but I've never known him to be a bushwhacker."

"He bushwhacked me, Sheriff, but only killed my horse!"

The sheriff had his .45 out and demanded, "Hand over that hog leg, cowboy. I'm puttin' you in jail until the judge gets back to town an' can hear your case."

"I killed him in self-defense. It was either me or him."

"The judge will decide that, cowboy. Now just turn around and head back into my office. Might even try you for horse stealin' too. That alone is a hangin' offense."

Tom turned and went back inside with the sheriff following.

"Step in that cell over yonder. I have to do some paperwork on this killin'. What's your name, cowboy?"

"Name's Tom Sikeston."

"Where do you hail from, an' how old are you?"

"I'm twenty-seven, from Elko, Nevada."

"You're a breed, aren't you?"

"My mother was Shoshone."

"What are you doing in this part of the country?"

"I'm workin' for the Bar-0-1 Ranch down on the Jordan River, rounding up cattle, movin' 'em an' brandin'."

"Well, it looks to me like you've been doin' more than workin' with cattle. Appears you're pretty handy with that six-gun."

"When's the judge going to be in town? Sure like to explain my side of the story."

"Judge should arrive here in a couple of days. You'd better have some kind of proof of your innocence. He doesn't cotton to Indians either. He thinks the only good Indian is a dead one."

"I don't think the color of my skin should have anything to do with it, and I don't know how I'm goin' prove my innocence when nobody was around."

"It looks like you're in a heap of trouble, cowboy."

How am I goin' to get out of this mess? As far as I know nobody was around during the shoot-out. Maybe someone at the dance saw this man ride out or maybe talked to him. Perhaps even the girl I was dancing with could shed some light on this whole affair. Nothing I can do right now but wait for the judge to come to town an' hope he'll believe my story. With what he thinks of Indians it doesn't look none too good. I might as well get some shuteye, as it's for sure I ain't going anywhere right away.

He had no more than dosed off when he heard the cell door open. It was the sheriff with a tray of food.

"Thought you might be on the hungry side so brought you some vittles from the hotel." He set them down on his bunk.

"Much obliged, Sheriff, as I'm on the hungry side."

"Received a telegraph from the judge an' he should arrive on the stage day after tomorrow."

"Sheriff, could you send a telegraph down to Jordan River and maybe find someone who saw the shootin' or knows the reason this man was gunnin' for me? If you would have someone go down there or ride down there yourself, my tracks should be easy to follow back to my dead horse and you'd be able to see he'd been shot."

"I'll send a telegraph first thing in the mornin' but don't see how that would help. As far as ridin' down there, I don't have the time but I'll see if someone will go down."

The sheriff turned around and Tom could hear the metallic sound of the key turning in the lock. It was the sound of freedom being taken away. He was wishing now he'd have just left the man's body lying out there on the sagebrush flats. *That wouldn't have worked either, as they would have found his body and my dead horse.*

He spent a terrible night looking up at a ceiling. He was used to looking up at the stars. He jumped off his cot as he felt something crawling on him. It was a big cockroach and almost big enough to throw a saddle on. He was sleeping fitfully when the opening of the cell door awakened him.

"Here's your breakfast, cowboy. Soon as the telegraph opens, I'll send the message you requested. Don't see how it will help you, as most folks around this town believe you killed young Charlie for no reason. I am of a mind to believe the same thing. I've known him since he was a young sprout. Little wild sometimes, but never seen him get into real trouble. I am surprised you brought him in though. Might help your case some, but I doubt it."

He turned and Tom could hear those boots thumping across the wooden floor to the front door and then the closing of the door to the street. He felt like a caged animal. He'd never been behind bars before. It was a terrible feeling. *Just hope the judge believes my story.* It seemed like this day would never end and he still had the night to go through. During the day he spent the time watching a bug scurry back and forth on the floor, and once in awhile a mouse would scamper in and check to see if there were any crumbs on the floor. When the first day ended he heard the sheriff open the door to his cell with his supper.

"Brought your supper, Tom. There's been no word from Jordan River yet. Might not hear a word before morning. The judge will be on the morning stage."

"When will I be able to speak with the him, Sheriff?"

"Not till the hearing an' that'll be in the afternoon."

Tom ate his supper and settled down the best he could for another long night. He had hopes the judge would believe him. He had no witnesses, so he realized he was in a bad spot.

The rays from the morning sun were streaming through his cell window, casting shadows on the opposite wall. Shortly the sheriff came with his breakfast. "Here's a little grub for you, cowboy."

"Has the judge arrived yet?"

"It's eight now. The stage should arrive around ten if they don't have any problems."

The sheriff left and Tom spent the next few hours pacing back and forth. It must have been about two in the afternoon when the sheriff returned. He unlocked the cell door, came in, told Tom to turn around, and proceeded to put handcuffs on him..

"There's going to be a preliminary trial in the judge's chambers where the judge will hear your case."

"Have you heard any word from Jordan River yet?"

"Not nary a word so far, maybe later today. Let's get along to the hotel for the hearing."

The Idaho Hotel was used for holding court since there wasn't a regular courthouse. It was a short walk on the boardwalk to the west and around the corner. Their boots on the boards gave out a hollow sound, like thumping on a half filled whiskey barrel, as they walked. They climbed up a narrow, steep flight of stairs to the room that was used for all legal matters, whether it be for land disputes or shootings. They entered a door to one side of the judge's bench. The sheriff knocked, and a voice from within bellowed out, "Enter."

The sheriff opened the door and a short, fat man with a goatee, black frock coat, and red- checkered vest with a gold watch chain dangling from one pocket to the other one, was seated in a overstuffed chair.

"Judge Potter, here's the man that is responsible for the shootin' of young Charlie Benson," announced the sheriff.

"I see. How are you, McCrea?"

"Just fine, Judge, and how have you been?"

"Fair to middlin', McCrea, fair to middlin'." He pulled a long black cigar out of his vest pocket, bit the end off and spat it into a brass spittoon next to his chair. He turned to Tom and asked, "Well, young man, what have you to say, an' what tribe do you belong to?"

"I am half Shoshone and it was self-defense, Your Honor. He shot my horse out from under me an' then just missed me with another shot. I lay in a gully until he rode down off a hill. When I stood up, he drew but I was faster, and my shot killed him. I never found out why he was gunnin' for me."

"Doesn't look to me like you are in a very favorable position. Young Charlie was a highly respected young man around these parts. He has a lot of friends in this part of the country and Indians are not all that welcome around here. So far you haven't given me any reason why I shouldn't indict for murder. We'll set the trial for one week from today. That'll be June fifth. You can take the prisoner back, Judd. We'll get together later for a drink."

"We'll surely do that."

Tom spoke up, "That's not giving me much of a chance, Your Honor."

"More of a chance than you gave young Charlie. Get him out of here, McCrea."

These Indians are nothing but trouble to us. They should make 'em all stay on the reservation, Potter thought as they left.

"All right, Tom, let's get you back to the jail."

"What about a lawyer? Ain't I entitled to one of those?"

"You'll get a lawyer. I'll talk to Stubbs tomorrow and see if he will take your case. He's the only one we have. You might have a chance with him, but the only problem, Charlie used to run a lot of errands for him. He'll be the only one you will be able to get especially for the pay the county hands out. Could get one out of Boise but that would take money."

"I don't have any money. All I've been is a workin' cowboy, never did much of anything else."

They walked back into the sheriff's office and he motioned for Tom to turn around. He took the handcuffs off, pointed to the cell, and once again the metal sound of the key turning in the lock seemed to echo his doom.

"I'll see you in the morning; don't run off now."

Tom didn't think he was very funny and didn't like the sound of the lawyer that would apparently take his case. It looked like it would be an open and shut case against him. *I've got to see if the lawyer will ride down to Jordan River and see if he could find someone who can clear me. Have to wait till morning to see. Might as well settle down for the night and see if I can sleep.* He had a very fitful night, but before he knew it, he was brought some breakfast. He could sure use that black coffee.

"Sheriff, will I get to see this lawyer, Stubbs, today?"

"I'll talk to him later today an' see if he'll come over and talk to you about your case."

"I need to talk to him as soon as possible if my trial is in one week."

"Don't be irritating me now, cowboy. I'll get to him soon as I get the time."

He turned and walked away, shutting the door between the cells and his office.

I better be thinkin' of another plan if this lawyer can't get me off. Might try escapin' but right now I don't know how that could be possible. Just keep my eyes open for a chance. Wish now I'd stayed in Elko, but this was a good job at the Bar-0-1 spread. If I ever get out of this mess I'll stay away from pretty country girls. Just have to wait till I go before the judge I reckon, Tom thought.

He woke up to sunshine shining in his eyes. He stood up, walked over to a table, and from a wash pan filled with water, splashed some on his face. He reached up for a dirty, stained towel hanging on a nail, and dried his face and hands. He felt somewhat better as it awakened him. He turned and the sheriff was there with breakfast.

"I see you didn't run off, cowboy."

"I don't care much for your humor. Let's trade places."

"I have to fun you some, Tom. This afternoon the lawyer will be in to see you. His name is Vernal Stubbs."

"That's the best news I've heard since being in this hell hole."

Judd turned and left. Tom's breakfast consisted of some sowbelly, beans, a slice of bread, and black coffee that surely hit the spot. He could hardly wait for the lawyer as he only had six more days before the trial. He began to go over in his mind everything he could think of to tell this Stubbs.

Must have been around two in the afternoon when McCrea and a tall, skinny man with a bushy salt and pepper moustache and a baldhead that looked like it had been polished from the way it shone, walked in. The cell door was opened and the man walked in. He stuck his hand out, and Tom, not wanting to offend, took the offered hand.

"Name's Vernal Stubbs, young man, and I already know your name. Let's sit down on your cot an' you can give me all the information you can think of."

Tom proceeded to tell him everything and asked him, "Mr. Stubbs, can you ride down to Jordan River and see if you can find that girl, or someone else that knew the man I shot? And maybe find out why he rode out on those flats to shoot me? We had been coming up short on cattle. Maybe he was tied into that and was afraid I was gettin' close to findin' out who the rustlers were. Maybe the girl knows something about it."

"Do you know the girl's name?"

"If I remember right her name was Corrine. Never found out her last name."

"Very well, I'll ride down first thing in the morning and see what I can find out."

He stood up, put his hat on to cover most of his baldhead, and yelled out at the sheriff to come unlock the cell door.

"I'm done questioning the suspect for the present, McCrea."

"Vernal, I'm going over to the hotel an' have a bite to eat with the judge, care to come along?"

"I'd like to, Judd, but I have some pressing business that requires my immediate attention. Some other time though."

Judge Potter was at the hotel sitting over by the window overlooking the front street with the prosecuting attorney, Will Buttrow. Buttrow had thick gray hair hanging down to his shoulders and a beard down to the second button of his shirt. His eyes were sort of squinted with a mean look in them. He looked like a mountain man instead of a lawyer. The judge spotted McCrea as he came through the door and motioned for him to come over.

"How are you this evenin', Judd?" the prosecuting attorney asked.

"Couldn't be better, Will. How was your trip to Boise?"

"The wife and I had a very enjoyable time and took in the play *Hamlet* while we were there, an' last but not least, dinner at D'Vitos. Superb. Now what do you think of this upcoming trial of the half-breed you're holdin'? I think he's guilty and will try to see he hangs. I was fond of young Charlie, nice boy."

"I have the same feelings myself, but being the judge I must be impartial."

"I agree, you must do your job," responded Judd.

"Vernal isn't too keen on Injuns so it will probably be a quick trial because I don't believe he'll put up much a defense," retorted Buttrow.

"It's getting a little late for me, boys, so I believe I'll head home," the judge said, as he pushed back his chair and stood up.

Tom was sitting there watching that mouse sneak out, grab a crumb of bread and scamper back under the cell door. *Right now, mouse, I'd like to change places with you, but I reckon you wouldn't stand for that. Hope my attorney goes down to Jordan River and finds out something that can help me. I have nothing to do but wait till tomorrow because it's for sure I ain't goin' anywhere.*

Vernal saddled his mare, Poppy, and headed for Jordan River. Riding between sagebrush hills, he startled a big mule deer buck. It took off up the hill and disappeared into some pine timber. Vernal was following a creek lined with poplars, willows and green grass growing up the slopes a short distance on each side of the stream. It meandered through the hills eventually dumping into the Jordan. As he rode along he was thinking, *Don't know why I'm wasting my time because I believe he's guilty, but I have to put up some effort or I won't get paid.*

He arrived in Jordan River and rode to the front step of the mercantile. There was a short porch in front and a bench for old timers who had nothing to do except swap Injun stories and do a little whittling. It was empty today. The store was the only building around except for a small barn a hundred yards or so down close to the river.

He dismounted and entered. Behind the counter seated in a rocker was an old man with a white beard that reached to his belly button. He was sound asleep and rocking the place with his snoring. Vernal tapped the counter with the butt of his gun and the old man came alive.

"What can I do for you, young man?" he asked as he slipped his glasses on. "Oh, Mr. Stubbs, I didn't recognize you without my specs."

"I'm down here on a investigation matter, Hezabyah. There's a young man in jail in Silver City that claims he knows a girl down here that might clear him of murder. I'm looking for a girl by the name of Corrine; don't know the last name. I have never heard of her myself."

"There was a girl by that name visitin' at the MacNuff ranch on the Owyhee River. That'd be ten—twenty miles from here. I've never been too keen on calculating distance. Fact of the matter is I heard she went back to Missouri where she came from."

"Was there someone else at the dance that you recollect?"

"I believe Karl Bever was there. He lives down this road a short piece. Maybe he can tell you something."

"Thank you, Hezabyah, for the information. I'll ride down there and talk to him."

It was a short ride to the Bever ranch, maybe two miles; arriving, he turned up a long lane lined on each side with big locust trees. The ranch house had aspen trees along the sides, and juniper trees in front. A man saw him coming and was waiting on the long porch that ran the full length of the house.

"Hello, stranger, you look tired. Climb down off that horse and rest yourself a spell."

"Thank you, don't mind if I do. This riding is beginnin' to take a toll on me, my age and all."

"Sit down in that rocker yonder and tell me what I can do for you."

Vernal got off old Poppy, took the man's offer and sat down in the rocker.

"Would you care for a drink, whiskey perhaps?"

"That would suit me just fine."

"You just make yourself at ease and I'll bring us a shot of whiskey." He brought the bottle and poured each of them a generous shot and then told the lawyer, "You're on the Karl Bever spread and I'm the owner, Karl Bever. What can I do for you?"

"Mr. Bever, I am down here investigating a shooting. There's a man in jail by the name of Tom Sikeston who shot a Charlie Benson. Claims it was self-defense. I understand you were at the dance so I thought maybe you could throw some light on this. I'm Tom's defense lawyer."

"Don't know if I can help you much 'cept I knew Charlie and he could be a little hot-headed sometimes. I think he was a mite jealous of this new girl visitin' from Missouri. I didn't really know Tom, 'cept I knew he rode the range for the Bar-0-1 Ranch southwest of here. I believe he left the dance at almost daylight, and shortly after that Charlie left. Never paid no mind where they were goin' but thought they were headed back to their jobs. Don't know who Charlie worked for or even if he worked. I figured him to be a bit on the lazy side. Don't think he cared too much about hard work."

"I'm obliging to you, Mr. Bever, for the information. I'll be getting back to Silver City before it gets dark."

He walked out, swung up on his horse and said to himself, "I'm getting too old for this horse backing. Time I get a buggy. I guess the only defense I can give is self-defense. Don't think it will hold water though. Trial shouldn't last over one day and I can get back to my regular chores. This would be fine for some young, upstart lawyer just out of school. Only problem is I'm the only defense lawyer in town."

His horse was just plodding along with her head hanging down low and Vernal doubted the old bay mare would be around much longer, but she came to life when a horsefly lit on her rump. She was hopping down the road like a young filly and Vernal was trying to stay in the saddle.

"Whoa now there, Poppy!" Vernal yelled out.

CHAPTER 2—TOM AND JAIL

I wonder if my lawyer was able to find out anything. It's late so don't expect my lawyer to come see me today. Sure do hope he's found out something. Only three days 'til the trial, and I have to think of a way to escape should my trial go bad. I just don't know how it would be possible right now to get out of here.

He was sitting on his cot thinking all these things when he heard the door open. It was the sheriff with some grub.

"Sheriff, have you seen my lawyer this evenin'?"

"I saw him ride over to the hotel. Expect he was going over for some supper."

"Do you think he might come see me this evenin'?"

"Can't say whether he will or not. Best you eat your supper before it gets cold. If I see Mr. Stubbs, I'll tell him you would like to see him."

"Thank you, Sheriff."

McCrea turned and left, shutting the door behind him. Tom felt like a caged lion. *If I ever get outta here they'll not get me back. Course I won't be if they hang me, but I don't intend for that to happen.*

He finished his supper and lay back on his bunk. He threw a piece of bread on the floor so he could watch that mouse. In a sense they had become partners, as they were both in jail. Here he comes! *This time, just sitting there eating the bread. Not afraid of me anymore. Might as well settle in for some sleep.*

He was sleeping soundly when he awoke with a jolt. He looked around—yes—he was still in jail, but at least he was alive. He had been dreaming and what a horrible dream it had been. He dreamed he was standing in a crowd of people watching a hanging. He looked up, and it was his own body swinging gently from a rope.

He sat there on his bunk as the rays of the morning sun bathed his cell with orange colors reflecting off the morning clouds, and the bars on the window casting shadows on the floor. As he sat there contemplating his fate, he turned and the sheriff was turning the key in the lock, bringing him his breakfast.

"Here's some grub, Tom. I saw Mr. Stubbs over at the hotel having breakfast and he said he would see you later this mornin'."

"Did he say if he went to Jordan River and found out anything?"

"No, he didn't say anything about his trip, except he had sores from riding over there. He'll probably tell you everything when he sees you."

Tom said no more and began to eat his breakfast. *Sure do hope the lawyer comes in soon.*

Tom finished his breakfast, and must have dozed off when the creaking of the cell door awakened him. It was the sheriff and his lawyer. McCrea turned around and went back out, shutting the other door.

"How are you this morning, Tom?"

"I'm tired of this place an' want to get out. Did you find out anything?"

"I am sorry, I couldn't find anyone that knew anything. The girl Corrine has left and went back to Missouri. The only defense we can give is self-defense. Don't think you have much of a chance. Maybe we can call on the mercy of the court and get you off with life in prison."

"That's not much comfort."

"I'm sorry, Tom, but we don't have any proof that Charlie was out to kill you, or anything about rustling."

Stubbs left and Tom started planning on how he was going to escape. He could see now it was his only chance.

About two more days till the trial. I will just have to wait and watch for a chance out of here.

The cell door opened and the sheriff entered with another man. Tom recognized him.

"Hello, Pete, I've been wondering when someone from the ranch would wonder where I was and come lookin' for me."

Pete was a short, stocky man with a bushy black moustache. He was around five feet eight with a neck like a bull and wore a buckskin shirt and buckskin pants. A little leather bag hung around his neck. He never said what was in the bag except the contents kept the fever and evil spirits away. He was the type of man that if a bull had you in a corner, he could be depended upon to get you out. He never gave his last name and spoke with a French-Canadian accent. Never said where he came from, more and likely had Indian blood.

"What's goin' on, Tom? The foreman, Frank Colter, sent me out to the south range to see what had happened to you. You hadn't came in to the ranch house and he thought maybe you had taken off with some steers, as we have been missin' quite a few head. I found your dead horse an' took your saddle and rifle back to the bunkhouse."

"Pete, this Charlie Benson shot my horse from out from under me, from a hill a hundred yards or so from me, then came down to finish me off. We had a shootout and he lost. I thought the right thing for me to do was bring his body to town. That's when they arrested me for murder. It was plain self-defense. I think he may have been one of the rustlers and figured I was getting close to findin' out who it was. My trial is goin' to be held about two days from now.

"Pete, can you ride down, look around and see what you can find out? The lawyer rode down to Jordan River to talk to the girl that I was dancin' with at the dance but found out she went back to Missouri. The shooter was at the dance and actin' mighty jealous of her. The lawyer also talked to Karl Bever, who was at the dance, but he couldn't help."

"I'll ride down there today and see what I can find out. If I can't find out anything I might just have to bust you out of here. Looks to me like the sheriff, judge and lawyers are all crooked in this town. I have heard of that judge and they call him the hangin' judge like the one in Texas. Don't believe you're goin' get a fair trial. We'll have to figure out a way to get you out. I'm goin' leave now, Tom, ride down in that country where you was workin', and check some of those canyons. Might even find some missin' cattle," Pete replied.

"I'd be obligin' to you, Pete. Wish I was goin' with you, but as you can see I'm a little indisposed."

"I will be back day after tomorrow. I know that ain't much time, but can't be helped."

"Alright, I'll see you day after tomorrow."

"Sheriff, I'm ready to leave," he yelled.

McCrea opened the door and Pete left.

"Is your friend goin' to see if he can find out somethin' that would help you?"

"Don't know what he could do, as he doesn't know anything about why I was shot at." *I don't want the sheriff to know anything because, for all I know, he might be tied in on the rustling.*

CHAPTER 3—PETE

Pete was headed to the south range where Tom's horse had been shot out from under him.

I believe I'll ride over to those canyons to the south of where the shooting took place. Be a good place to hide cattle. Problem is they may have already moved 'em. There's the chance I can find tracks and follow 'em if it hasn't rained. That would have covered up any sign. There have been some clouds over that way but don't know if it rained.

He worked his way through the sagebrush until he came to the edge of a canyon. *Don't see any cattle from up here. I'll ride down that side over by those junipers. Looks like an easy way down.* He started down, and it was steep. His horse almost sat on his butt and slid part of the way down. When he got to the bottom he started riding down through the small pine and junipers looking for sign. It looked like it had rained some. *Don't know if it washed out any tracks or not. I'll keep riding down this canyon to see if I find any. Whoa, what do we have here? A whole passel of tracks and they sure ain't buffalo. Ain't been any of those critters in this part of the country in twenty-five years or more. I can smell cattle. It's gettin' late so I better set up camp for the night and start out early in the morning.*

He made camp in a grove of poplars, with a scattering of scrub pine, sagebrush and juniper. *I best build a small fire 'cause I don't wish to alert any rustlers if they are around. Should be well hid here. In the morning I'll see where these tracks go. Might as well settle in and get some rest.*

It was quiet except for the hooting of a owl and the baying of a coyote in the distance. Most creatures had settled down for the night except the night prowlers. Once in awhile the flapping wings of a night bird broke the silence.

He spent a restful night and was up early, built a small fire, brewed himself a pot of coffee, had a little jerky and saddled up. He found the tracks and started following them down the canyon. Just before topping a rise he heard cattle bawling.

I better tie my horse up and sneak up to where I can see.

He crawled on his belly through the sagebrush to the top where he could look down. He could see cattle. Must be a hundred to two hundred head down there. *Don't see anyone except a cowboy sitting over on the hill to my left. I need to sneak down and take a look at those brands. Looks like I can get close enough by going down that creek. With all the brush and the gully he won't be able to see me.* He got to the bottom and there was a bunch of cows getting a drink from the creek. *I recognize those brands and they're stolen. I see some Bar-0-1 brands too. Now I need to sneak around behind that lone rustler and get the drop on him.* He worked his way back to where he had tied his horse and rode where he could get behind the cowboy. Pete got off his horse and crawled to where he was behind the rustler. *Appears he's asleep.* He managed to get close enough and stuck his pistol in the man's back.

"Don't try to be a hero cowboy and you'll live. Very gently lift your six-shooter out with your left hand and hand it back to me."

"Who are you and why are you sneakin' up on me?"

"I think I should be the one asking questions. Who are you and what are you doin' with those cattle?"

"Name's Ben Ross and I was just watchin' these cattle for the owners."

"Now just who might the owners be? I would say half the ranchers in this part of the country. Who you workin' for, and I want straight answers or I'll dig you a grave out here!"

"I work for Frank Wollen."

"Where's he now?"

"He and Andrew are out bringin' more cattle."

"Where are the cattle goin' and who else is involved?"

"I don't know except someone important in Silver City is involved. They don't tell me anything."

"When you expect this Frank and Andrew to be back with more cattle?"

"Don't rightly know and that's the truth. Could be this evenin' or maybe tomorrow. They'll be with this next bunch. They planned to drive 'em over to Boise and sell 'em, hoping to have at least three hundred head. Right now cattle are bringin' a good price."

"Do you know a Charlie Benson?"

"No, not personally, but I know he was workin' for Frank, helpin' with all this."

"I can't wait till your friends come back. I have a friend in jail and he is goin' to stand trial for the murder of Charlie. It was self-defense. We're going to town and you're goin' tell the judge what you know. Might help Tom."

"I don't know. I heard the sheriff and the judge was tied up in this rustlin'."

"It looks like we have a problem then."

"We'll take a chance that Tom's lawyer is not involved. You can tell your story to Stubbs. Mount up, we're goin' to town. Put your hands on the saddle horn so's I can tie 'em. Don't try anything because I won't hesitate shootin' you."

Pete led Ben's horse back to where his own horse was tied. They swung into their saddles and rode for Silver City. They worked their way over to the road that went from Silver City to Jordan River, kicking up a cloud of dust as they rode along at a slow lope for a spell, so as not to tire the horses. After they had ridden a good distance, they reined the horses into a walk. He wanted to be far enough away from the cattle in case some of the rustlers came back.

"Don't know who we're goin' to tell your story to since the sheriff and judge are both in on this rustlin'. How about Will Buttrow, do you think he might be involved too?"

"I don't know about him. He could be."

"I believe we'll tell your story to Vernal Stubbs. We have to trust someone."

"Why don't you let me go? They'll probably kill me and I wouldn't be surprised if Vernal Stubbs and Will Buttrow aren't involved too. I won't have a chance."

"Well, Ben, don't worry yourself, as I'm going to keep a close watch on you. They won't get to you, if I can help it. We'll go straight to Stubbs' home. We won't get into Silver City till dark. We'll ride around the backside of town to Stubbs' so we won't be seen. I see town ahead of us now."

Stubbs' house was just on the other side of town. They didn't see anyone as they rode up to his house. There was a light shining in the window. They tied their horses around back where they wouldn't likely be seen. Pete dismounted and told Ben to get down. He untied his hands. They walked up to the front door, knocked, and a voice within hollered out, "Who is it?"

"This is Pete, a friend of Tom's. I have someone with me that might help clear Tom."

"Just a minute while I unlock the door." Vernal opened the door and Pete and Ben walked in. "Who is this you have with you? Can't say I know him."

"This is Ben Ross. He is a part of a rustlin' gang, and Charlie Benson was in on it also. I found him guardin' a bunch of cattle. This may come as a shock to you, but he claims the judge and the sheriff are in on it."

"That's a big charge. I've never known Judd and Judge Potter to ever do anything outside the law. Don't know as how I can believe this story. You go find a place to bunk down for the night and I'll mull this over."

"You best have it thought out come mornin', cause we're goin' to be back and you'd better be ready to do something."

"Don't be a threatin' me, cowboy! I'm all you've got to help get Tom resolved of this charge."

"Alright, we'll see you in the mornin'."

"Ben, we'll go down to Martha's roomin' house and get a room.

She's one we can trust. Her place is just outside of town so I don't think anyone will come nosin' around. Don't try to escape from me. I just as soon shoot you as not."

They rode out to the edge of town to Martha's. The building was weather worn, as she didn't believe in wasting any paint on the outside. In fact her yard matched the house, all cluttered up. It was said she was a good cook though. Pete had never eaten there. They tied their horses around back so they would be hidden from view. "We'll get our room and then take 'em to a stable," he told him. They made their way through all the obstacles in the yard to the front door and knocked. A short stout woman came to the door.

"You act normal and don't try anything," Pete whispered to Ben.

"What can I do for you, boys?"

"Ma'am, we need a room for the night if you have one."

"I do, and that will be two dollars, one room upstairs for the both of you, includin' breakfast in advance."

"That'll do just fine."

"Breakfast at seven."

"We'll take care of our horses, ma'am, and come back."

They walked out, mounted up and took the horses to the livery barn. They walked back to the boarding house a short distance away. When a cowboy has to walk in his boots he sure enough doesn't want to travel very far.

When they arrived, Pete told him, "Alright, Ben, let's get on upstairs."

Their room was right at the top of the stairs. Pete opened the door and motioned for Ben to go on in.

"Sorry to have to do this, cowboy, but I'm goin' to have to tie you. I'll make you as comfortable as possible, but I ain't takin' any chance of you runnin' off or cuttin' my throat while I was asleep. Lay down on the bed and put your hands behind your back."

Pete tied his hands and run the rope down and tied up his feet also.

"Might as well get as much sleep as you can. I'm goin' to lay down beside you and get some sleep myself."

Wasn't long before both were snoring. In the morning there was a knock on the door.

"Time for breakfast, cowboys," Martha called out.

"Much obliged, ma'am, we'll be down directly," replied Pete.

"You keep a tight lip, Ben. I wouldn't hesitate shootin' you right in this house."

"I'll keep my mouth shut, I promise you that."

They walked downstairs to a hot breakfast. They could smell the smoked bacon, eggs and homemade biscuits. Neither of them had anything like in quite some spell, being out on the range. They sat down and filled their plates.

"Eat hardy, cowboys. Don't want to throw any out to the hogs."

"Mighty tasty vittles, ma'am. Don't get this kind of food out brandin' cattle."

"You boys goin' to be here tonight?"

"I reckon we will, ma'am. We have some business in town."

"We'll let the horses feed and rest all day. We'll more than likely have to spend another night here, Ben."

They walked to the livery barn and told the hand working there. "Give our horses grain and hay. We'll be back later."

"I'll take good care of 'em," he replied.

They left the barn and headed for Stubbs' house.

"I see another horse there at Stubbs'. I don't recognize it and I don't like it. We've got to go in though." They walked up to the door and knocked and Mrs. Stubbs came to the door.

"Vernal is waiting in the parlor. Go right on in," the wife told them.

They walked in and were mighty surprised as who was there. It was the sheriff.

"What is he doin' here? This was supposed to be between you an' me."

"I didn't really believe your story, and thought Judd ought to be here to hear your accusations. I never thought for a minute the sheriff and judge were mixed up in any rustling. I do believe it's called slander and you could be sued."

"I don't know why you think Judge Potter and myself are involved in anything illegal. I don't even know this young man you have with you," the sheriff replied.

Ben spoke up, "I wasn't doin' any rustlin', Sheriff. I was just ridin' through the country and stopped to rest an' fell asleep. First thing you know this cowboy snuck up behind me and stuck a gun in my back."

"You're a liar, Ben. Shoulda known you cut an' run. You don't care if an innocent man hangs for somethin' he did in self-defense. Just want to save your own skin."

"I won't arrest you this time, Pete, but I'd advise you to leave town today. If I catch you around this evenin', I'll arrest you for sure. As far as you're concerned, Ben, I'm takin' you into custody as a material witness."

"You are lucky the sheriff is takin' you to jail, because I would have taken care of you out on the range."

Pete walked down, retrieved his horse, saddled him and headed out of town. He had to make a plan to break Tom out of jail. *At least the sheriff will think I'm gone and won't be causing any trouble. Don't have any idea what to do just yet, but I'll come up with something. I'll ride on back to the ranch. Maybe someone might consider helping me.*

He rode through the hills, among the junipers and pine timber, and rode down along the creek weaving in around the poplars, staying concealed as much as possible. There was the chance someone would want to get him out of the way. He arrived at the ranch and went directly to the main house and found the foreman, Frank Colter.

"Found Tom, and he's in jail in Silver City, Frank, accused of murder, but it was self-defense. A man by the name of Charlie Benson tried to kill him but only killed his horse. They had a shoot-out and Tom came out on top. He was getting' close to findin' out about the rustlin' that's been goin' on. I went back out and found his dead horse and brought his saddle and rifle to the bunkhouse. You weren't here. I decided to look in some of those canyons south of here and found about two hundred head of cattle and a man named Ben Ross guarding 'em. I snuck up on him, got the drop on him and took him into town. He claimed the man Tom shot, Charlie Benson, was involved in the rustlin' along with Judge Potter and Sheriff McCrea. I took him to talk to the defense lawyer but he double-crossed me and brought the sheriff. The sheriff arrested Ben as a material witness so they called it. Don't believe his life is worth a plug nickel, but he don't matter because he'll lie in court anyway to try and save his hide."

"When's the trial, Pete?"

"Tomorrow. We've got to do something, maybe break him out."

"We'll go sit in and watch the proceedings, Pete, an' see if we can figure out what to do. Maybe take a couple of the boys from the branding crew with us. You ride out to the south range and bring in Harvey and George. Best have 'em here come early mornin' so's we can be in town by trial time."

Pete headed out to the south range on his roan gelding, a horse that made good time without tiring. He had been riding hard for most of an hour when he topped a gray-back ridge, scared up a bunch of antelope, and could see the cow camp just below in a small valley. It was late evening but there was still plenty of daylight as he rode into camp. There were four men working here on this range branding and earmarking calves and cows. As he rode up Harvey hollered at him, "What are you doin' out here, Pete? Thought you were working the range southwest of here."

"I was, but Tom has got himself in a passel of trouble, and is in jail for shooting a man that tried to bushwhack him about a week ago. The sheriff in Silver City threw him in jail for murder. His trial starts tomorrow. I found rustled cattle being guarded by a man down one of those canyons in the southwest. I got the drop on him and he spilled his guts to me. He told me the sheriff and judge were involved. Frank wants you and George to go with us to town. We need to ride back to the ranch house tonight and we'll all ride in tomorrow. Have to find a way to break Tom loose. You know Potter is called the hangin' judge."

They cut out some fresh horses from the remuda. Harvey and George saddled up and told Pete, "Let's ride."

They headed back to the ranch headquarters, arriving just as a full moon was rising over the distant mountains. There would be four of them riding into town in the morning.

They were up early. The cook had breakfast fixed for them. After they ate, they mounted their horses and headed to town. It would be impressive, four of them riding in. They were all tough cowboys who knew how to use a gun and a rope.

CHAPTER 4—TOM'S TRIAL

Tomorrow's the day Tom reminded himself. Sure hope Pete was able to find out a way to clear me or get me out of here. It was a bad night. Don't believe I slept an hour. Come to think of it, I didn't see that mouse. Smart, he was probably checking out somewhere else where he could get a free meal.

The outer door opened and McCrea was coming with his breakfast. The metallic sound of the turning of the lock as the sheriff opened his cell door echoed in Tom's ears—another night behind bars.

"Here's your breakfast, Tom. In a couple of hours I'll be taking you over to the hotel for the trial. I'll be back after you finish up," he said as he turned around and walked out.

Tom didn't say nary a word as there wasn't anything to say right now. When the sheriff returned he opened the cell door and told Tom to turn around, while he put handcuffs on him.

"Alright, Tom, let's get on over to court."

There was that familiar sound again, boots on a boardwalk sounding like thumping on half-empty barrels as they walked. The sheriff's big Mexican rowels on his spurs were making a jingling sound. Tom was still hoping Pete and some of the other hands were coming up with something that would free him.

They walked up the steps to the courtroom. McCrea directed him to the defense table and sat him down.

"I'm goin' take the handcuffs off you, Tom. I'll be sitting right here behind you."

The courtroom was filling up with people who wanted to see the outcome of this trial. Most knew Charlie and expected this cowboy to hang. Tom turned and saw Stubbs walking through the door. He was headed for the defense table.

"Good morning, Tom. How are you this morning?"

"I ain't none too good, seein' how the deck is stacked against me."

"I'll do my best with what evidence we have. I'm afraid that Ben Ross wouldn't have been a credible witness. The sheriff is holding him somewhere but don't know where. He sure ain't in jail. If I can locate him I might put him on the stand. Might have to force McCrea to produce him."

The prosecuting attorney walked up to the defense table.

"How are you this fine morning, Vernal?"

"Couldn't be better, Will, and you?"

"I expect this will be a short trial, Vernal, don't you reckon?"

"Most likely but it depends on how the jury looks at it."

"You got something up your sleeve, Vernal?"

"You never know, Will. Like to keep you guessing."

They all turned as the bailiff announced, "All rise." Everyone stood up as Judge Potter walked in, took a step up to the judge's bench, and motioned for everyone to sit down.

"Bailiff, instruct the spectators there'll be no smoking or spitting in the courtroom."

With his gavel he hit the table and said, "This court is now in session. The State versus Tom Sikeston on the charge of murder, date June 5, 1876.

"Go ahead, Will, give us your opening statement. Tell it to the jurors." There were six men seated to the left of the judge's bench.

"Thank you, Roy. The State says the man seated at the defense table shot young Charlie Benson in cold blood, never gave him a fighting chance. He claims self-defense but he has no proof. I don't see we ought to waste the court's time. We should find him guilty and get on with sentencing."

"And what do you say to these charges, Vernal?" the judge asked.

"I believe, Roy, there are circumstances that couldn't be helped.

I knew young Charlie and he was a fine boy, but maybe he lost his temper, challenged Mr. Sikeston and forced him to draw."

"I object, Judge, it was plain, outright murder," replied Will.

"Objection overruled. Let Vernal state his case."

"Well, I believe, Judge, it was an accident. I don't believe he intended to kill Charlie. Maybe his gun went off accidentally."

"I object again, Your Honor. Guns don't go off accidentally."

"Objection sustained, Vernal. You've got to come up with something better than that."

"Alright, Judge. I'd like to call Mr. Sikeston to the stand."

"Go ahead, Vernal."

"Take the stand, Tom," replied Vernal.

Tom walked up to the bench, sat down in a chair and the bailiff told him, "Raise your right hand, put your left hand on the Bible and repeat after me. I promise to tell the whole truth and nothing but the truth so help me God." Tom repeated it and was told to sit down.

"Alright, Tom, tell the court just how this killing happened."

"Like I told you before, this Charlie tried to gun me down. Shot my horse first, then drew his pistol, but I was a mite faster and he lost. I didn't intend to kill him but he forced me into it."

"Had you ever seen him before all this happened?"

"Yes, at a dance down at Jordan River. I was dancin' with this girl and this young man was actin' kinda jealous. I didn't think too much on it and left."

"I object, Roy. I don't believe it's related to the case."

"Overruled Will. You know in a lot of killings there's a woman involved."

"Vernal, you know he's guilty, why don't you just give up?" replied Will.

"He might be guilty of killing Charlie but maybe—just maybe he was forced into it."

"Alright, you two, let's get back to the trial," the judge reprimanded the lawyers.

The four riders from the Bar-0-1 were just entering town. They were a tough bunch of cowboys. No men would want to tangle with them, not even lawmen. Harvey and George stood about six feet and were as wiry as a piece of rawhide. Each carried a .44 Winchester and a Colt .45 Peacemaker. The foreman wore a Remington Army .44 and a .44 Winchester rifle. There was no one in the streets when they rode in. Those who weren't at the trial were staying home.

They rode up, tied their horses to the hitching rail in front of the hotel, dismounted and walked in where the trial was being held. They pushed the courtroom door open, strode in and were met by the sheriff.

"You cowboys will have to remove your pistols until after the trial. The bailiff will hold 'em."

They unbuckled their guns and did what they were told, even though they were not fond of the idea. They found themselves a seat and the trial continued. Tom saw his friends from the ranch and that made him feel a whole lot better. The trial proceeded.

"It's your witness, Will."

"Thank you, Vernal."

"Step on back up here, Tom. You've already been sworn in so no need for that again."

"Mr. Sikeston, how can you possibly call it self-defense? We don't even know if young Charlie carried a gun. When you brought him in, there wasn't a gun."

"He had a pistol and rifle. I brought his rifle in on his horse. I don't know what happened to the pistol. Must still be out where my dead horse is."

"We don't have any proof of that. I think you gunned him down in cold blood and would have left him there, but you were afraid if you didn't bring him to town, your horse would have been found and it would lead the law right to you. I also think you probably shot your own horse to make it look like it was self-defense."

"I object, Your Honor," replied Vernal. "Will is badgering the man."

"Sustained. Will, stick to the facts. I don't want to be here all day. Let's get on with it."

"Sorry, Your Honor. I'm done with him for the time being."

The judge struck his gavel on the desk and announced, “Court recessed for thirty minutes. Will and Vernal, I want to see both of you in my office.”

The courtroom emptied and the spectators headed for the saloon to get a drink. The two lawyers followed Judge Potter back to his chambers.

“Shut the door behind you, Will,” the judge ordered.

“Will, you and Vernal have to stop this wrangling around an’ get down to business. This trial shouldn’t take over one day. If you don’t carry this on, I might be able to give this cowboy an easier sentence, but right now you’re wearin’ on my patience. Now that I have spelled that out for you, let’s have a drink before we go back in the courtroom.”

“That sounds mighty pleasing, Roy,” remarked Vernal.

“I’ll second that,” Will said.

The judge reached into a drawer, brought out a bottle of his best whiskey, three glasses and poured a drink for all. They finished their drinks and filed back into the courtroom.

“All rise,” the bailiff announced.

When the judge seated himself, he motioned all to do the same.

“This court is now in session. The Honorable Judge Roy Potter presiding.”

“All right, Vernal, proceed,” ordered the judge.

“Thank you, Judge. I would like to call Ben Ross to the stand, but the sheriff has him in custody somewhere and I do not know his whereabouts. I want him to produce him.”

“I object, Your Honor. I don’t believe he has any bearing on this case.”

“Overruled, Will. We have to give the defendant every legal chance possible. McCrea, I want you to bring Ben here. We will go on with the trial till you get back.”

“It will take me about an hour, Judge.”

“Well, all right then, get to it. Don’t want to be here forever.”

The sheriff left the courtroom, walked down to the livery barn, saddled his bay gelding and rode out of town. He arrived at a weathered old shack where he was keeping Ben Ross. One man was guarding him. He stepped down off his horse, walked up to the front door, knocked and a man within opened the door with a pistol in his hand.

"Hello, Sheriff, you come out to check on the prisoner? Hasn't given me any problems whatsoever."

"I have to take him into town, Dan. The judge insists I bring him in. Wants to give the accused man every chance."

"Do you think he can cause us any problems, Judd?"

"He'll be warned that if he says the wrong thing it will be his death sentence. Go bring him out of the back room. I have to get back to court as quickly as possible."

Dan brought Ben out and McCrea told him, "We're goin' into town to the trial and you will be put on the stand. You keep your mouth shut about any rustlin' or about Charlie gettin' killed. You know nothin'. You want to live so this will just be a formality to please the judge and Stubbs. After it's over, you'll be goin' back to tend to the cattle."

They mounted up with Ben's hands tied and his horse being led by the sheriff. When they arrived at the hotel they had been gone just a little over an hour. They walked in and Judge Potter remarked, "You certainly took your time, Sheriff. You should have been keeping him in jail."

"I figured, Judge, he would be safer somewhere besides jail."

"Alright then, let's get on with the trial. There's your witness, Vernal."

"I wish to call Ben Ross to the stand," replied Vernal.

Ben took the stand and the bailiff instructed Ben to place his left hand on the Bible and swear to tell the whole truth.

Ben replied, "I do, so help me God."

"Ben, where were you on the night of the alleged killing?"

"What do you mean alleged killing? We know there was a murder committed," Will called out.

A lot of voices in the room echoed their sentiments also and loudly.

Judge Potter was banging his gavel on the desk. "Order in the court or I will empty it. Will, try to restrain yourself on these outbursts. This is not a circus."

"Go ahead, Ben," replied Vernal.

"What was the question again, Mr. Stubbs?"

"Try to pay a little more attention, Mr. Ross," Vernal told him as he repeated the question.

"Don't know where I was the time of the killin'."

"How do you come to be here in the first place?"

"That cowboy in buckskins brought me in at gunpoint and the sheriff locked me up in some cabin out of town."

"What were you doing to cause him to bring you to town?"

"Like I said, I was just passin' through, stopped to rest, was off my horse sittin' there and admirin' the view and cattle grazin' down below me and fell asleep."

"Whose cattle were they?"

"I object, Your Honor. There has been a killing and that's what the subject should be, not cattle. It's not related."

"Sustained; Vernal, stick to the facts of the case. Will is right. This is a murder trial."

"Judge, I'm trying to prove there's a connection. My client mentioned rustling."

"You will have to come up with more than what you have so far, Vernal."

"Do you wish to cross-examine the witness, Will?"

"Yes I do, Your Honor."

"When you are working, Ben, what is your normal occupation?"

"Sometimes I work at brandin' cattle or most any work I can find."

"More like brandin' someone else cattle," Tom remarked.

"Vernal, instruct your client to keep his mouth shut," replied the judge.

"Did some one sneak up on you while you were asleep, stick a gun in your back and take you to town to Stubbs' house? What he was doin' was taking you hostage so to speak, wouldn't you say?" the prosecuting attorney asked Ben.

"I would say so and first thing I know a gun is stuck in my back. There was cattle down below us and he claimed they were stolen."

"Is he in the room now?"

"Yes, he is sittin' right there behind Mr. Stubbs and the defendant."

"That's all I have for now."

Vernal asked, "Do you wish to question Ben again?"

"Yes, I do."

"Just stay right where you are, Mr. Ross," the judge said.

Vernal walked up to Ben, turned around, walked over, and stood in front of the jurors, then asked, "How can you prove you were just taking a nap while passin' through the country? Can you produce someone that could vouch that you were just traveling through the country?"

"I can't say that I know anyone who could verify what I have said since no one was with me."

"You're admitting there was cattle around, so how do we know they weren't stolen?"

"I object, Your Honor. I thought this was murder trial and not a rustling trial."

"Sustained. Vernal, I warned you to stick to the facts. The cattle mentioned have no bearing on this case."

"Very well, Roy, but I think they could very well be important and maybe help my client."

"That's all the questions I have for him at this time."

"You may step down, Ben, and remember you are still under oath.

"I was hoping this trial would be over today, but I can see it will not, so I am recessing until tomorrow at 9 a.m. Court adjourned," the judge announced.

CHAPTER 5—TRIAL ENDS

The spectators all filed out, heading for the bar and a drink before going home. Pete and his friends walked out, mounted up, and headed for Martha's rooming house.

"Don't look like Tom is gettin' a fair trial, but I think we should wait till we hear the verdict before we decide what to do. If they decide against him and the sentence is hangin', then I suggest we break him out of jail. It will be tough as they'll certainly send a posse after us, an' I say we'll fight," Pete told them.

"If we have to break Tom out, I think we should head for the ranch. They'll think twice before goin' into Oregon. They will have to contact authorities in Burns and that will take some time, and under the circumstances the law there may not want to travel to Jordan Valley with a case such as this, especially when they are informed of the crooked law and justice system in Silver City," suggested the ranch foreman."

"Let's get on up to the roomin' house and get a room and some chuck. I'm downright on the hungry side. Don't know about you, cowboys," George commented.

"Sounds like a good idea," remarked Harvey. "It's been a long dry spell since we left the ranch. I think it would be downright proper to go down to the bar and have ourselves a drink of whiskey. What do you think, Frank?"

"We'll do that right after we rent a room and have supper."

They arrived at Martha's, tied up their horses at the hitching rail in front and made their way through all the junk to the front door. Pete knocked and Martha came to the door.

"What can I do for you, cowboys? Need a room and vittles?"

"Yes we do, ma'am. Can you oblige us?"

"Most certainly. I have two rooms available. You'll have to double up. Supper is almost ready and should be on the table in thirty minutes. The two rooms are at the top of the stairs and to the left. That's two dollars for each room and that includes supper in advance. Breakfast is extra. Twenty-five cents each."

"Sounds fine to us, ma'am," Frank replied.

The four Bar-0-1 hands walked up the stairs to the rooms to wait until it was time to put the feedbag on. They were a bunch of hungry cowboys who hadn't eaten since early morning. "Soon's we eat, let's ride on down to the livery barn and then to the bar for a drink. I'm as dry as a seven-year drought," Frank said.

"That sure does sound mighty pleasin' to me," Harvey remarked.

"Right smart idea," George chimed in.

"Should be about time to eat I'd wager. Let's get on downstairs," Frank told them.

Pete remarked, "Martha is a fine cook."

"That she is, as I can tell by the smell driftin' up the stairs," replied Frank.

They sat down to a family-style dinner of steaks, steaming hot mashed potatoes, vegetable, hot sourdough biscuits and coffee.

"This surely does beats the beans, jerky and hard biscuits we have to eat while we're out brandin'," the cowboys remarked.

The men finished their meal and walked to the local bar where many other townspeople were having drinks and talking about the trial. The men at the bar turned and looked at this tough looking bunch of cowboys who had just walked in. They could hear the jingle of spurs and rustling of well-worn leather chaps.

"What'll you cowboys have?" the barkeep asked.

"Just bring us a bottle of whiskey," Frank told him.

The bartender brought the bottle and four glasses and asked Frank, "Are you boys friends of the defendant?"

"That we are and it looks like you have a crooked judge here, and his only interest is to see an innocent man hang."

"He always seemed to be a fair and honest man to me. He has kept this town a right safe place to live. He don't take no nonsense from any hoodlums tryin' to ride rough-shod over the decent citizens here abouts."

After hearing those comments, the four walked over to a table to finish their drinks.

CHAPTER 6—McCREA

After court had recessed for the day, the sheriff went to Judge Potter's home.

"What are you going to do about this Ben Ross, Sheriff? What if he talks and folks in this town go checkin' some of those canyons where the cattle are?"

"Don't fret yourself too much, Judge. He ain't goin' say a word because he values his health, and besides, I've ordered the cattle moved to market soon as the rebrandin' is done and we get our hands on other hundred head or so."

"Well Judd, that does make me feel somewhat better. We've got to watch Vernal though. I think he is beginnin' to enjoy this trial and maybe wants to pursue the rustlin' bit more. Will, on the other hand, I believe could be bought. He hasn't always led a straightforward, honest life. He's been known to turn a crooked card now and then. Might pay to have a little talk with him, Judge."

"Not at this point. We'll see how the trial goes tomorrow."

"Alright then, Judge, I'm goin' to have supper, and I have to feed the prisoners. I put Ben in an adjoining cell. Since he's in this trial, thought it would be better to have him close and behind bars so I don't have to worry about him runnin' out."

"I'll see you tomorrow at the trial, Sheriff."

The sheriff walked over to the hotel for supper and to buy food for the prisoners. As soon as he finished eating he took the meals to the jail. He opened the outer door, walked in and set the food down on his desk before opening the door to the cells. He then picked up Tom's meal and took it in.

"Thought you boys might be gettin' hungry."

He unlocked Tom's cell and put the tray down, went out, and locked the cell. There were just two cells. He then took Ben's supper to him and started back out to his office when Ben spoke up. "Why are you keepin' me in here, Sheriff? Nothin' I can do in this trial. I've already told all I know."

"You're still a witness and Vernal may want to put you on the stand again. Don't see how it would help Tom much, as you didn't see him gun down Charlie unless you're holdin' back something."

"Ain't holdin' back a thing, Sheriff. I've told all I know."

Tom was listening to all this. *I wonder if he is tied up in the rustlin'. Haven't been able to talk to Pete so don't know what he has found out. So far it doesn't look too good for me. Hope Pete has an ace in the hole, as right now I'm holdin' a dead man's hand.*

"You boys best get some rest for the trial tomorrow. I'll be bringin' your grub at six in the mornin'," the sheriff told him, interrupting his thoughts.

"Ben, did you see me shoot Charlie Benson? If you know anything I could sure use your help."

"Don't know why they're keepin' me, as I don't know nary a thing. I hope they turn me loose tomorrow so's I can get on out of the country."

"If you're lying about something that could help me, you know my friends will hunt you down and you won't live to see another summer."

With that said, Tom laid down on his cot. He decided to get some rest and be prepared for tomorrow.

Tom spent a restless night and had just dropped off to sleep when the sheriff came in with their meals.

"Alright you cowboys, time to jump up and have a little grub before we head for court. I'll be back shortly."

Tom and Ben were both hungry and didn't need any coaxing to down their food. Shortly after they finished McCrea came back in, took the plates and coffee cups and went back out to his office. He returned with a man he had sworn in to be his deputy for the time of the trial.

"You boys come on out. It's time we head back to the hotel for the trial. This is my deputy Caleb," the sheriff told them.

Their hands were handcuffed behind their backs, and they headed for court. The courtroom was already filled up with townspeople, miners, and cowhands. The sheriff and his deputy removed the handcuffs.

"Sit yourself down there at the defense table, Tom. Caleb, take Ben and sit him down behind Tom."

Will and Vernal had just entered through the door and were headed for their tables.

"Good morning, Tom. Hope you are in better spirits today. We won't give up. I haven't had a case like this in years."

The judge entered and the bailiff motioned for all to rise. Judge Roy Potter sat down and motioned for all to be seated. He banged his gavel on his desk and announced, "This court is now in session. Vernal, who would you like to call to the stand?"

"I would like to call Pete, the wrangler for the Bar-0-1."

Pete walked up and took the stand and repeated the oath.

"What can you tell us about Tom and this killin'?"

"I have known Tom for quite a spell, and I know he wouldn't kill a man unless he was forced into it."

"Objection, Your Honor. What can this man possibly tell us that would change it from plain murder to self-defense?"

"Sustained. Vernal, what are you trying to do here?"

"I'm going to try to prove rustling had something to do with the killing."

The judge hit the desk with his gavel, apparently angry.

"This court will take a five minute recess. Vernal and Will, I want to see you in my chambers."

They followed the judge back and shut the door behind them just as the judge exploded.

"What're you trying to do, Vernal? This is a murder trial. Has nothing to do with this buckskin heathen."

"I agree; there's no connection," replied Will.

"I'm sorry, Roy, but I believe rustling has everything to do with the murder."

"Very well, but you had better give the court some solid proof."

They filed back into the courtroom and the judge told Pete to take the stand again.

"Alright, Pete, tell this court what you know about the rustling and how it could be tied to this shooting."

"Mr. Stubbs, after findin' that Tom was in jail and talking to him about it all, I decided to ride out, find his horse and maybe do a little lookin' around for myself. I did just that and found rustled cattle just beyond his dead horse in a canyon. That's where I found Ben Ross."

"I object, Your Honor. I don't see any connection."

"Sustained. Vernal, instruct your witness to stick to the facts."

"Judge, I'm trying to prove there is a connection between rustling and the shootin'."

"I'll allow it this time but be careful."

"Very well. Pete, what else can you tell the court?"

"Mr. Stubbs, I found Tom's horse, and it had been shot in the chest. His rifle was underneath. It was quite a chore to retrieve it, but I managed it. I took both that and his saddle back to the ranch."

"That'll do for the present, Pete."

"Your witness, Will," replied the judge.

Will turned, stroked his beard, looked towards the spectators and asked Pete, "How can you be sure the horse was killed by another man? Couldn't he have shot his own horse after he murdered Charlie?"

"I don't believe he did."

"Just answer the question yes or no."

"No."

"What makes you think he didn't shoot his own horse?"

"Because he loved that horse and he wouldn't shoot any horse unless they had a broken leg or somethin' like that."

"All indications point to murder and besides, Pete, I think you would say anything to help your friend."

"I know Tom, and he killed that man because he had to."

"I don't believe that for one minute. I'm through with the witness, Judge."

"Do you wish to question the witness, Vernal?"

"I do, Judge.

"Pete, how long have you known Tom?"

"Most of a year now."

"Have you ever known him to be dishonest with anyone?"

"I object, Your Honor. What does that have to do with the case?"

"Objection sustained. Vernal, stick to the facts."

"Very well, Roy. I just believe these things have something to do with the case."

"Pete, you say you snuck up behind Ben, got the drop on him, and he admitted he was involved with rustling?"

"Yes, and he named names."

"Who were they?"

"He named Judge Potter, the sheriff and some cowhands."

The courtroom spectators began talking loudly to each other after that remark. The judge hit the table with his gavel, demanding silence and said, "Quiet or I'll clear the courtroom. I think we have heard enough. The jurors will retire to another room and decide if this man is guilty of murder or not. They will disregard what they heard about rustling and stick to the facts of the case. I declare this court in recess until the jurors reach a verdict. Until that time, Will and Vernal, let's retire to my chambers for a much needed drink."

Back in the judge's chambers, the first thing out of Judge Potter's mouth was, "Vernal, are you accusing the sheriff and me of rustling?"

"Not exactly, Judge. Just trying to get facts to help my client. I would hope you're not in involved in such a thing. This is what Ben Ross told Pete."

"Would you take the word of a drifter over mine?"

"That's a serious accusation, Vernal," replied Will.

"I'm not sayin' you're into rustling. Just repeating what Pete said. I don't really believe you and the sheriff would do anything illegal," Vernal came back.

The bailiff knocked on the door. "Open," replied the judge.

"The jury is back with a verdict, Judge."

"Thank you. We'll be right in."

The three of them filed back in and the spectators stood up until the judge sat down.

"I understand you have reached a verdict. Let's hear it," the judge said.

"We find the defendant guilty of murder, but maybe he had to act in self-defense."

"Tom, stand up while I pronounce sentence. Under doubtful circumstances I sentence you to ten years in the territorial prison. Tomorrow the sheriff and four armed guards will deliver you."

Tom wasn't surprised. He didn't really expect anything different since the lawmakers were crooked. He would have to depend on Pete and the other riders from the Bar-0-1 to help him escape.

CHAPTER 7—OFF TO PRISON

Pete and the riders from the ranch were talking among themselves.

"I knew this was goin' to happen," Pete remarked.

"Let's get out of here an' do some plannin'," added Frank.

The four of them left the hotel, swung aboard their horses and rode down to Martha's to rent rooms for the night. Then they gathered together to discuss how they would break Tom out.

"I think we could waylay the posse up at the pass. They'll be expectin' somethin' but I believe we can do it. Have to watch the sheriff though. Heard he's good with a gun," Pete said.

"If we can pull this off, I suggest we hightail back into Oregon. The sheriff doesn't have any jurisdiction there and it would take quite a spell for him to contact the Oregon authorities," remarked Frank.

"I say we hit 'em where it hurts. Find those rustled cattle, steal 'em, then hide 'em out or drive 'em to market. Doubt if they have had time to move 'em," suggested Harvey.

"Here's what we'll do," Frank told them. "When we break Tom loose, two of us will try to throw 'em off the trail while the other two will take him back to Oregon an' hide him out until we get there. There's goin' be a whole lot of shootin' so if anyone one wants out, now's the time."

"We're all together in this. If it had been one of us, Tom would have done what we're doin'," said Frank. "I doubt if they'll leave before ten in the mornin' but we best be out of here early and waitin' for 'em."

"I think it would be better if I take Tom and join my friends, the Nez Perce," Pete remarked.

"Maybe that would be better," replied Frank.

The judge had called Sheriff McCrea up to his house to talk about moving the prisoner.

"Do you figure you'll have any trouble from any of the Bar-0-1 boys that were in town, Judd? Word has it they'll still around."

"I'm expectin' trouble but we can handle it. I believe if they're goin' to try anything it will be at the pass. We'll surprise 'em. We won't go that way; instead we'll take the trail that goes up and around the mountain. By the time they realize they've been tricked we'll have made enough distance they won't be able to catch us."

"I think you ought to see that Tom has an accident before you get to the prison."

"I'm figurin' on that, Roy. I'll have to shoot him because he attempted to escape."

"Have you sent word to the boys to hurry on the brandin' so the cattle can be driven to market?"

"I sent Ben Ross back to work an' told him to get it done."

"I'll rest a whole lot easier when Tom is six feet under and the cattle have been sold."

"Now don't you fret yourself, Roy. Everything is goin' to be just fine. Before you know it, we'll be back in business again collectin' more cattle for the market. You can rest easy tonight."

Vernal Stubbs walked over to the jail, entered, and told the deputy guarding Tom he wanted to talk to him in private. Tom looked up as he entered.

"Open up the cell, Caleb. I want to talk to my client."

"Can't do that, Stubbs; sheriff's orders. You'll have to talk to him through the bars. I'll shut the other door so you can have privacy."

He went out and closed the door and Vernal told Tom, "I'm sorry I wasn't able to get you off with a lighter sentence, but I didn't have enough evidence. I'm on your side, Tom, and I agree with you, Ben is a liar. I promise you I'll work to get you freed. I think you may be right. Maybe the judge and the sheriff are connected with rustling."

"I'm sure of it. I can't do anything about it right now, but I can promise you I'll be back, unless I'm murdered before I get to prison."

"I have to go now but rest assured I'll be working on your behalf."

Vernal opened the door and left.

If and when I get out of this, there's going to be some people that'll wish they had let me go in the first place. I'm not even sure about my lawyer. This is something I'll have to take care of, Tom thought.

The outer door opened again and Sheriff McCrea walked in with Tom's evening meal.

"We'll be leaving for the prison in the morning sometime so you best get a good night's sleep. It's going to be a hard ride and you'll be well guarded. If your friends try to interfere they'll meet with a lot of hot lead."

"I may have to serve ten years, but I'll be back and you better hope you have died of old age because you will be dead of poison—lead poison."

"I don't believe you're much of a threat, so I won't worry myself any too much over it."

Judd turned and walked out, shutting the door behind him.

It was a long night, but morning came and McCrea entered with Tom's breakfast.

"Eat up, Tom. We'll be leaving sometime this mornin'."

I don't have any appetite today, Tom thought, *but I better eat anyway. On the trail I'll have to be prepared for anything. Wouldn't be a bit surprised if Pete and the boys have a welcoming party for the sheriff and his paid crooks.*

He was lying on his bunk when he heard the sheriff enter with a couple of deputies.

"Time to go, Tom. Put your hands out. I'm goin' handcuff your hands in front of you. Don't attempt to escape because you'll never make it."

With Tom securely in handcuffs, they walked out to the horses, mounted up and headed out of town. The sheriff and two deputys, Ty and Ralph, were in the lead with Coker and Matt riding in the rear. Sheriff McCrea had a halter on Tom's horse and he tied the lead rope to his saddle.

"You boys keep a sharp eye out. Should be at the spot soon where we'll go around the mountain instead of over the pass. I expect his friends could be layin' in wait for us somewhere's around that area. We're goin' fool 'em and go around—longer, but I believe safer. I expect those four cowboys at the trial will be the ones that'll try to ambush us."

CHAPTER 8—BAR-0-1 HANDS

"You know, Frank, I have a gut feelin' the sheriff will avoid the pass. There's that trail that goes around the mountain—farther, but a better chance for him to sneak past us. Don't know how many men he'll have with him."

"Pete, we're ahead of 'em so I suggest two of us take the trail and find a good spot for an ambush. If shootin' is heard either from the pass or the trail, the other two, whomever it might be, will hightail as fast as they can to help out."

"Sounds good, Frank. Harvey, you and George set up a ambush at the pass."

"Alright, Frank, let's get to ridin'."

The two men took off up the trail and rode till they found what looked like a favorable spot to waylay the sheriff and his party. It was a spot with large rock outcroppings that would conceal them and give them an advantage. They dismounted and Frank rolled himself a cigarette. He had just finished the smoke when down the trail he spotted six riders.

"Pete, I see em comin'. You were right."

"When they get close to this spot, they're goin' to be mighty careful, Frank. Make those first shots count."

The posse could see a place comin' up that could be a good spot for an ambush. "I don't take those cowboys for fools, especially Pete. He has a lot of savvy," McCrea told them.

"Sheriff, I suggest we get down off our horses and walk," Coker said.

"You may be right. Let's dismount."

They left Tom on his horse and they walked slowly, taking a good gander at those large rock outcroppings.

Frank and Pete could see the posse had dismounted. "They're being cautious or just plain smart," Pete whispered.

"Pete, I can't tell for sure who's the sheriff. I have a feelin' if we get a couple of 'em, the rest will cut and run. They're just townsfolk and not much for gunfights."

"You take that skinny one on the left, and I'll take the fat boy beside him, Frank."

They waited till they were about a hundred yards from them, then started shooting. Deputies Matt and Coker went down. The others were scrambling for cover. Frank and Pete had them pinned down.

Down at the sheriff's end, it was pandemonium. Matt was hollering, "I'm hit, McCrea. They got me in the leg."

Coker was moaning. "I'm shot. I need help, Sheriff."

"You boys just hang on. I'll get to you soon as I can. Ty, you and Ralph work your way around those rocks; see if you can get behind the shooters. I'm goin' to work my way up through those junipers on the mountain."

Sheriff McCrea was down on his hands and knees crawling up through the rocks, making his way around the junipers and sagebrush. *If I can get over there on that ridge I might be able to get a shot at 'em.* He managed to get over there, but one of them spotted him and took a shot but missed. They had him pinned down. *Maybe Ty and Ralph will be able to get into a position so as to take the pressure off me.*

Pete spotted the sheriff as he reached the ridge and took a shot at him.

"The sheriff is over on that ridge to the right of us, Frank. Took a shot at him but missed. If Harvey and George heard the shootin' they should be here shortly."

"Let's keep the pressure on the two below us, Pete. I reckon if we can nick another one they'll cut and run, maybe even the sheriff too. I see Tom's off his horse and crouchin' among those rocks. Never know, they might just decide to shoot him where he stands."

About that time one stuck his head out behind a rock and Pete took a shot. He heard a holler.

"They shot my ear off, Ralph. Don't know about you but I'm gittin' outta here. Tom isn't worth gittin' killed over."

"I agree with you, Ty. What about Coker and Matt?"

"Maybe when we get back down to the trail, we can help them on their horses."

"Sheriff McCrea ain't goin' like it."

"He's a good man with a gun. He can take care of himself. Let's go."

The two beelined for the trail and managed to get there without hearing nary a shot.

"Matt, we're gittin' outta here. For what we're bein' paid it ain't worth getting' shot or killed. We'll help you on your horse."

"I agree with you, Ty. Let's help Coker on his horse. He's bad off. Don't know if he can make it to town and the doc."

They loaded him on his horse and started riding down the trail back to Silver City. The sheriff couldn't see them so he didn't know they lit out. He yelled over to Pete and Frank and told them, "You boys may as well give up. We have you surrounded."

"Don't rightly think so, sheriff. If you take a gander, you'll see your boys hightailing it. There are four of us against you. The other two should be here any minute. You ride out of here and we'll let you live," hollered Pete.

Judd maneuvered around where he could see, and sure enough his deputies were riding out. *I can see I don't have much of a chance, but this ain't over. I'll ride back to town and raise a large posse, if I can find some men with backbone.*

"Alright," he yelled back. "You cowboys got the upper hand now, but you ain't seen the last of me. I'll find each and every one of you and you'll hang . I'm headed down. Don't shoot."

Pete was cautiously optimistic. "We best watch him, Frank, till he's out of sight. Don't know what he'll do when he runs into George and Harvey, but I think they have gone right over the mountain. I see McCrea has reached his horse. He's mounted up and headed out. Let's ride down and find Tom. Don't see him so he must be hidin'."

After a few minutes of sliding, dodging sagebrush, and working their way around through the junipers and scrub pine with their horses, they reached the trail.

"Where you be, Tom?" Pete yelled.

"Right here behind this rock, and am I glad to see you fellas. I knew you wouldn't let me down."

"Hey, boys, I see Harvey and George comin' over that ridge yonder," Pete commented.

They arrived and were glad to see Tom and to know he was in good shape.

"One thing we have to do, Pete, and that's get these handcuffs off. You know McCrea took off with the key."

"I know a man on over the mountain that has a little place, and I'm sure we can get 'em off, Tom."

The five of them mounted up and rode on over the mountain on a well-traveled trail that took them through scrub pine and down the other side to a small valley where a man by the name of Henry Fetterman raised fine horses and sold them to the U.S. Cavalry and to ranchers. As they entered the front gate a man met them with a rifle pointed at them.

"What's your business here, cowboys?"

"Henry, it's me, Pete."

"Pete, how are you? I should have recognized you with those buckskins. Don't have the eyesight I had when I was younger. How are you? Haven't seen you in a month of Sundays."

"Just been busy workin' cattle over at the Bar-0-1. We have a man that needs handcuffs removed."

"You fellas light down off them horses, come on in and I'll scare up some coffee. First off bring your friend over to the barn and we'll see if we can't remove those handcuffs. I won't ask what he's done as I expect you'll soon tell me."

They walked over to the barn and Henry told Tom, "Lay your hands down on that anvil. I'm goin' make a key of sorts that I believe will unlock 'em."

Tom did as he was told. It took Henry a little time but he eventually worked a thin piece of metal up in the lock, and before Tom knew it, the handcuffs were off.

"There you go, Tom. Ought to make you feel a sight better havin' them irons off."

"Sure does, Henry, and I'm beholdin' to you."

"Henry, Sheriff McCrea was takin' him to the territorial prison because of a killin' he did in self-defense. We waylaid his party and took him away from 'em."

"I know about the crooked judge and that sheriff, Pete."

"We expect he'll be back, and with a large posse, most likely through here."

"No need to fret yourself none as they won't get any information out of me," Henry said.

"Henry, we're goin' to have to get back on the trail and put some distance betwixt us and Silver City. We're obligin' to you."

"I'm glad I could be of some help to you, Pete. You keep your eye on your back-trail."

"We surely will, Henry."

The five riders mounted up and rode north. They needed to put some distance between them and any posse. After dropping down out of the mountains, they found a canyon that perhaps would be a safe place to make camp.

"We'll make camp over there under those bluffs, fellas. I believe we should find water close by and I don't reckon anyone will spot us. There's a grove of cottonwoods that ought to offer us some shelter," Frank suggested.

"I like the idea. My backside is tired from all this ridin' and my butt is galled," George remarked as he dismounted.

It was obvious he was hurting because of the small steps he was taking.

"Tom and me has been doin' some talkin' and we think it best we ride north instead of goin' back to Oregon. I have some Nez Perce friends that would take us in. No one will give us any trouble," Pete told them. "We'd like to be in on findin' and stealin' the rustled cattle back, but we think this idea's the best."

"I'm beholdin' to you, Frank, and the boys for what you did for me. You can be sure it'll never be forgotten," replied Tom.

"We did it, Tom, because you would have done the same for any one of us. We best get some sleep. Tomorrow will be a long ride for the three of us and I reckon the same for you and Pete," Frank answered.

Just before dawn the clouds opened up with a downpour and bolt lightning. They found shelter, and set up camp next to the bluffs. The cottonwoods gave them shelter from the driving rain. They built a small fire, brewed a little coffee and ate some hardtack. Their exit out of town was so fast there wasn't time to buy anything.

"Frank, when you ride back, you be mighty careful you don't run into McCrea; don't expect he'll just pass the time of day with you," Tom said.

"We'll skirt around Silver City. Don't reckon he'll take a chance on comin' into Oregon, but if he does we'll take care of him. He knows he has no jurisdiction there and is not liked. We hope to see you and Pete sometime. You've always got a job at the Bar-0-1."

"Much obliged for that, Frank. Hope the day will come when we can return. I'd like to even the score with that sheriff, an' the judge too," replied Tom.

The cowboys parted company and headed out on their separate trails. The sky was overcast and threatening to rain again. A cold wind was picking up and blowing tumbleweeds at them as they rode along. They sunk their heads down in their slickers to keep the wind and rain out.

"Tom, let's ride down in the canyon and get out of this blowing wind. I believe we best not go through Boise because the sheriff might have telegraphed them to be on the lookout for us."

"You're right. They wouldn't get me without a fight though."

They entered the canyon at the shallow end. There was a trail used by Indians and wildlife. A small creek ran through it with some poplars mixed in with the sagebrush.

"We'll ride north through Indian Valley and on up to Council Valley where we might find my Nez Perce friends, Tom. In the short time I've known you I've wondered if you had an Indian name."

"My mother's people call me White Eagle because I'm half white."

They were riding north through a large valley northwest of Boise and entered low rolling hills covered with sagebrush and no timber, and down to a long valley with bunch grass up to a horse's belly.

"This would be a fine place for cattle, Pete, but reckon we can't be thinkin' about that right now. McCrea might have contacted Boise and maybe they might send a posse or the cavalry out to look for us."

"This is big country, Tom. I doubt they would be much concerned about us, except we'd better watch out for the cavalry. Although they are probably busy watching the Nez Perce right now, and I've heard there might be war. The whites are taking too much Indian land and want to put 'em on reservations."

"That's the way it's been all over, Pete. Bad for me because they consider me the same as full blood."

"Tom, those clouds look none too friendly. Gettin' real black and movin' our way. Listen to that distant rumble. Don't know about you but I'm gettin' a mite chilled. We better find shelter. I see a place up yonder that ought to do. Looks like a cabin."

They rode up to the cabin and noticed smoke coming out of the chimney. It was a square cabin built out of pine logs and a sod roof. Somebody had taken up residence here, maybe a trapper. They rode up to the front, the door opened and a grizzled old man was facing them with a rifle. "Who're you men and what're you doin' in these parts?"

"We're just cowhands travelin' through, heading north, old timer. We'd like to get in out of that approaching storm," Tom told him.

"Alright then but don't try anything. Light down off those horses and come on in and warm yourselves. There's a corral behind my cabin where you can put your horses."

They led the horses around back, unsaddled them, and went on into the cabin. They stood before the fireplace warming their backsides and it felt mighty good. The old man began to warm up to them somewhat. It was obvious that he missed the company of other human beings.

"I've got some beans on the fire and a young buck I killed this mornin', iffen you're hungry. I was fixin' to have a bite when you rode up. I'll just add some more to the pot. Won't take long." He went outside to the side of his cabin where he had the meat hanging.

"That's right kind of you. We are a mite hungry," replied Pete.

When the trapper returned, Tom asked, "What do they call you, old timer?"

"Name's Wiley Smith. Most folks just call me Trapper Smith. Where you fellas headed? I do a little trappin' and it's been fairly good of late. Getting' quite a few beaver. Don't know if you boys have heard about the unrest of the Injuns here abouts and farther north. My thinkin' is they're about to go on the warpath. Hey now, looks like the grub is ready. You cowboys dig in an' get your bellies full."

Tom and Pete filled themselves a plate and Pete remarked, "This is a fine and tasty meal, Mr. Smith."

"You boys are welcome to bunk down here in the cabin. Looks like we might be in for a lightnin' storm."

"Thank you kindly, Mr. Smith, as we are a mite tired from all day ridin'. Like to get to Council Valley and maybe to Meadows by tomorrow night."

They bunked down on the cabin floor and before sunup the old trapper was up, had built a fire in the fireplace and had started fixing some grub.

"Grab yourselves a cup off the shelf there and pour some hot coffee. It ought to wash away the cobwebs from your head. Beans will be hot shortly and I made some sourdough biscuits. Hot sourdough biscuits set mighty fine in the belly. Believe you'll have good ridin' today. Looks like the storm changed its mind an' moved east over the mountains into Long Valley. Now there's trappin' country. Lots of beavers."

"We are obliged for your hospitality, Mr. Smith," Tom told him.

"You cowboys are most welcome any time you're in these parts," the old man told them. "It's about thirty miles or so to Indian Valley and maybe another twenty to Council Valley. There are a few settlers there. I know that Rafe Anderson would put you men up for the night. You tell him you're a friend of Wiley Smith."

"We surely will. We're obliged," Pete replied.

Tom and Pete saddled up and headed for Indian Valley. Easy riding. Low rolling hills covered with tall buffalo grass and sagebrush. Hardly a tree in sight and they were few and far between. They crossed one little creek before they reached the Weiser. The storm clouds had disappeared over the mountains to the east. Today was going to be a clear, warm day. Three hours riding brought them to the Weiser River.

CHAPTER 9—THE JUDGE

Sheriff McCrea arrived back in Silver City and went straight to Judge Potter's house. He walked up to the front door and knocked. Potter came to the door not looking very happy.

"Well, I see you lost the prisoner an' got two men shot up, one pretty bad. The doc is working on him now."

"We were ambushed, Judge. Besides, the townspeople you gave me as deputies didn't have the stomach for a fight an' cut an' ran. Don't believe we have any men in this town that's willin' to take a chance on dyin'."

"You better find some men with guts to go with you to bring Tom back. He and his friends might try to expose our rustling."

"Judge, the orders were that as soon as they stole that other large bunch, which would be another hundred head or so, they were to drive 'em to market."

"I know, McCrea, but things have changed. Don't know what those men from the Bar-0-1 are going to do. We've got to get rid of these cattle an' hold off on any more rustling 'til things cool down. You've got to get back on the trail of Tom an' the other ranch hands. Can't have 'em running loose now. See if you can find a few good men that have the belly to fight; if necessary, offer them a good salary. Get those men an' I don't care how long it takes! I'll find someone to take over your job while you're gone."

"Can you handle everything here, Judge?"

"Don't you worry none. I'll take care of what is needed while you're gone. Let's hold a meeting at the hotel an' see if we can find some men with backbone to go with you."

Sheriff McCrea walked around to the local businesses and notified them of a public meeting to be held at four that afternoon. The judge would be there also. When the time arrived for the meeting, there was a good turnout from the town.

The sheriff announced, "I need some good men who are not afraid to use a gun an' don't worry about gettin' shot at. We'll go after Tom an' whoever is with him; we'll bring 'em back dead or alive."

"What sort of pay is in this dangerous job?" one man asked.

"The judge hasn't decided what it'll be, but he promised it will be substantial an' a rightly good bonus if we bring 'em back, dead or alive. It doesn't matter."

Another man said, "I hear tell these cowboys are real handy with a gun. Don't think I'd care for the job myself."

A local businessman echoed his sentiments also. "I don't believe you have enough money to pay me to chance getting killed. I've got a wife an' kids to think of."

A man from the back said, "If the money's right I'll go. Can't have these hoodlums runnin' roughshod over us folks."

Some other men shouted that it wasn't worth the risk and they would stay in Silver City.

"I'll go with you, Sheriff," another one announced. "When do we leave?"

"We'll leave first thing in the mornin'. Get our horses ready an' load up on stores to take. Also, I want to mention that the army has been alerted so they'll be on the lookout."

"That makes three of us then, as I'll go too," a man seated at the back of the room said, raising his hand.

"That concludes this meetin'. Whoever wished to join us, step on up here, sign up an' be deputized," the sheriff said.

Not very many were interested in taking such a gamble, but a total of five men stepped forward to sign up. They would be in for a surprise since all the "outlaws" except Tom and Pete had slipped back into Oregon, and were planning on stealing the cattle from the judge's rustled bunch.

The evening was spent gathering supplies. The next morning they loaded up packhorses for the trip. The six men mounted up and rode out of Silver City.

Tom and Pete arrived at the Anderson Ranch and were met at the front gate as the rancher came in from his hay field.

"Welcome, strangers, you boys look tired." He was a friendly, hard working man. "Come on in an' have supper with us."

"Thank you kindly," replied Tom. "This is my friend Pete and my name is Tom."

"Where you fellas headed?"

"Just headed north," replied Tom. He didn't want to tell him the law was after them.

"Could be dangerous that way. The news is the Nez Perce are actin' up some. Could end up in an Indian war the ways things are goin'.

"You cowboys are welcome to spend the night with us and go on in the mornin'," Rafe Anderson told them.

"That's right kind of you, Mr. Anderson. We'd be obligin'," Tom said.

"I'm afraid you boys are ridin' into trouble though. The Indians are stirrin' up somethin' fierce lately. They have killed a few white settlers, so we have heard. You'd be better to hang around here for a spell and see what happens."

"We appreciate your concern but we'll be just fine," Pete said.

They settled down for a good night's rest and in the morning saddled up, again riding north. Before leaving they thanked the family for their hospitality.

"We should make it on past Council Valley and make camp at the Salmon River. We might run into the Nez Perce around there," Pete told Tom.

"How long has it been since you were with the Nez Perce, Pete?"

"About three years. Don't know what to think about this war talk though. If we run into rampaging braves we could be in trouble.

We'll be lookin' for Alokut, Chief Joseph's brother and his band. With them we'll be plenty safe. Judd McCrea won't take a chance takin' us, I'll guarantee that."

They were entering Council Valley and there were a scattering of ranches. A lot of rich meadow grass, a prized area. Not yet any sign of Indians. They left the valley, riding through some pine timber and entering a beautiful expanse of meadows. Real fine cattle country.

Tom took note and said, "Surely would like to have land here, and some stock. A man could build a cabin, get a wife, settle down and raise a family."

"I don't believe it's in the cards right now, Tom."

They entered timber again and Tom's horse snorted and his ears pointed forward, listening; Pete's horse did the same. There was something up ahead.

"Hold up, Tom. Might be a band of Indians. Best we sit tight and see if they've spotted us."

"I see 'em, Pete. Looks to be about a twenty or so comin' down off that timbered ridge over yonder, ridin' our way. See those fine Appaloosa horses they're ridin'."

"The Nez Perce are well-known for their Appaloosas. We'd be better to wait right here, Tom, and see what they have in mind. We might be lucky an' it will be Alokut's band."

They were fortunate, as it was. The band rode up and Pete greeted them in their language. Alokut recognized Pete and said, "It's been many moons since we hunted the buffalo together. It is good to see my brother again. Where are you going?"

"We were hoping we would find you. My friend is half Shoshone and was accused of killin' another man an' was sentenced to prison. Myself an' friends freed him from the white law an' rode here hopin' to find you. We would like to join you for a season."

"That is like the white man's justice. We are riding to Montana to hunt the buffalo. You are welcome to join us. You will be safe with us, but I must remind you we are nearly at war with the white eyes. They are trying to force us off our beloved Wallowa land and put us on reservations. We will fight. The long knives are our problem."

"The soldiers could be looking for us along with a sheriff an' his posse," Tom told Alokut.

"That is not good. Before we go to Montana, we are going back to the Wallowas. We will return soon with more braves and go hunt the buffalo," Alokut told them.

"We will ride to the Clearwater River an' wait for you there," Pete told him.

"That is good, my brother. We will find you."

CHAPTER 10—SHERIFF AND POSSE

Henry Fetterman saw the posse before they arrived at his place. He was expecting them. He was standing in his front door when they rode up.

"Who you chasin' now, Sheriff?"

"Henry, we tracked five horses to your place and I know they're the men we're after. One is an escaped prisoner. What can you tell me about 'em?

"Not much, Judd. They were here and left some time ago."

"What direction was they headed? One had handcuffs on. Don't suppose you noticed that?"

"No, can't say I did."

One of the sheriff's men was poking around the barn and noticed the anvil. He came back over where McCrea was and told him, "Sheriff, I think he took those handcuffs off Tom. He has the means there in his barn."

"What about it, Henry?"

"Havin' an anvil doesn't prove anything, McCrea."

"You best not be lying to me because if I find you are, you'll go to jail with the rest of the outlaws. What direction did they ride?"

"Well you followed their tracks here so you should be able to follow 'em agin', but since you might have trouble trackin' 'em, all I can tell you is, they headed north."

"Alright, boys, let's ride an', Henry, most likely you'll be seeing me again."

The posse headed out north and found the tracks again, just beyond Fetterman's ranch. They followed them for a few miles and one of the deputies in the lead spoke up. "Sheriff, the tracks have split up. Two goin' in an northwest direction and three headed due west."

"We can't afford to divide our number so I think we'll take the ones goin' northwest. It's a wild guess but I've a gut feelin' Tom and Pete are the ones ridin' in that direction. We'll follow these tracks an' at the next town have someone notify the army even though I sent a telegraph from Silver City," the sheriff said.

"Sheriff, I see where they made camp down near those bluffs yonder. There's just two sets of tracks," replied Dan Wilkerson, one of his deputies and tracker.

"It's gettin' late. I believe we'll make camp here an' get an early start in the mornin'," the sheriff told them.

The horses and packhorses were tethered between two cottonwood trees. They got a campfire going and one of the men called William Basset, the designated cook, was preparing the supper consisting of beans and some biscuits.

Wasn't long till it was ready and he told them, "Come an' get your bellies full."

"In the mornin', I want to get an early start an' gain ground on those two. I'm anxious to get this over an' back home," the sheriff told them.

"I can surely agree with that sheriff," one of the deputies remarked.

They were up early, had a quick breakfast, saddled up and back on the trail. They were riding and following the trail of two horses when the tracks disappeared.

"Looks like that rain we had last night covered up their tracks, Sheriff. I see where they rode down into that canyon. There's a game trail goin' down through there an' my guess is we'll pick up their tracks again if we keep following this trail," Dan told them.

"Alright, let's ride a little harder. I intend to catch 'em before too long."

They rode a couple of miles down the canyon and Dan turned in his saddle and yelled back to the sheriff, "I found where there has been a camp an' I would wager it was them. My guess they're about a day ahead of us."

When they arrived at the end of the canyon they found a trail leading up to the top and Dan announced, "I found tracks again, Judd, an' I believe it's the same two. The tracks have veered off an' headed more north."

"Well, fellas, I believe they're staying away from Boise. Makes me wonder where they might be headed, maybe into Indian country. I have a hunch they're headed to Indian Valley and on north. We'll have a full moon tonight so we'll make up some time by ridin' all night. Do you think you can still follow their tracks, Dan?" replied the sheriff.

"It will be a little hard until later when the moon's higher but I reckon I can do it, Sheriff."

Several hours later they rode over a rise and down below a sagebrush covered hill stood a cabin. It was late and smoke was rising out of the chimney.

"We better approach the cabin with caution. One of you sneak around and see if there are any horses behind."

"I'll go take a look," Dan said. He crept around back, found a corral with two mules and a horse in it. He got back to McCrea and reported, "Don't believe they're here."

"Let's ride on up to the cabin an' see who is inside. They might give us some information," McCrea said.

They didn't make it to the front door before it opened and Wiley Smith was at the door with his rifle.

"Who're you men an' just what you doin' here?" Wiley yelled out.

"Take it easy, old man. I'm Sheriff Judd McCrea from Silver City an' we're on the trail of two killers who escaped from us. I want to know if they stopped here."

"Matter of fact, two men did stop here yesterday, but I doubt if they're the ones you're after. Just cowboys on the move."

"Was one wearin' buckskins, Mr..... I didn't get your name."

"Name's Smith, Wiley Smith. Yes, one was wearin' buckskins. They seemed like real decent young men."

"Sorry to say but one is a killer an' the other is just as dangerous. Which way did they ride from here?"

"They were headed to Indian Valley an' Council Valley, so they told me. That's all I know, Sheriff."

"Much obliged for the information, Mr. Smith. We'll be on our way."

"Sheriff, it looks like we are gettin' close to catchin' up with Tom and Pete. I believe we're gainin' on 'em. We ought to be in Indian Valley in three hours."

"When we get to Council, maybe we can enlist the help of the cavalry, if they're around. We have to worry about Indians from Council on," the sheriff said.

The arrived at a hill just south of the Indian Valley where they could look down on the Weiser River and the valley. They rode on through to the north end until they found Rafe Anderson's ranch.

Opening the gate they rode up to the front of the house and dismounted. Mrs. Anderson met them at the door and inquired, "What can I do for you, cowboys?"

"Ma'am, might your husband be around? We'd like to know if two men came through here recently, headed north."

"I will send my boy here to fetch my husband. Martin, go fetch your pa."

"From the looks of you men, I would say you could use some vittles before you travel on. Would you like to have lunch with us?"

"That would be right kind of you, ma'am. I reckon we're a mite hungry," replied the sheriff.

They dismounted and went into the house to wait for her husband. He arrived a short time later driving a wagon hitched to matching bay geldings. He came into the house and the sheriff introduced himself.

"Mr. Anderson, I'm Sheriff Judd McCrea from Silver City."

"Pleased to make your acquaintance, Sheriff. What can I do for you?"

"Mr. Anderson, we are lookin' for two men, one a escaped killer an' his friend that is dressed in buckskins."

"Well, Sheriff, two men did come through here yesterday. Maybe the ones you're after. They were headed for Council Valley.

"You cowboys have lunch with us afore you leave.

"Ma, set some extra plates."

"Rafe, I already took care of that."

"We'd be obliged, thank you. Some home cookin' will be a nice change from eatin' on the trail. After we eat, we'll be on our way."

"What did these outlaws do, Sheriff?" he asked while they were eating.

"Well, sir, one killed an innocent, well-respected young man of the community an' the one in buckskins helped him escape from my posse. The killer is a half-breed."

"I hope you catch 'em, Sheriff."

"We best get on the trail an' catch up with those murderers. Thank you for your hospitality."

The posse saddled up and rode towards Council. Riding hard they could make it two or three hours. There were two large hills to cross that were scattered with oak, pine, and locust trees, down to flat farm country, on into Council. They descended to farming country and Dan Wilkerson said, "I see the town of Council in the distance. Hope we'll have some good news there."

CHAPTER 11—THE CLEARWATER

Tom and Pete were riding for the Clearwater, where they would hide out till the Nez Perce come. Then they would cross over the Lolo Trail to Montana to hunt buffalo. They were still riding the same horses they started out with. Tom was riding his buckskin gelding, and Pete on his roan gelding.

"I believe we'll be safe hiding there, Tom. Have my doubts the sheriff will even come this far."

"Not so sure about it, Pete. I'd wager he's a man that doesn't like someone to get the best of him an' he can't afford for us to come back there an' expose his rustlin'."

"I expect you're right. We better keep a watch out. I was thinkin', Tom, we could set up a camp thereabouts an' do a little huntin'. Should find some staples we need at Mt. Idaho an' buy a packhorse. We'll make camp at the Salmon River an' go on to town the next day."

"I see the river ahead, Pete. Be nice to rest a spell. We've been doin' a lot of hard ridin'. Time to let our horses rest."

They reached the river in about an hour and made camp. There were steep barren mountains on each side of them. The river came from the east through a gorge and then turned north. There wasn't much vegetation and a small amount of timber on the north slopes. Not a good place to be, but they could see quite a distance to the south so if the posse was spotted, they might have a chance to escape. No telling how far the sheriff was behind them. They had to expect anything.

"Looks like a favorable spot over yonder behind that large rock there by the river," Pete said.

"Ought to be fine. Let's get a fire goin' an' brew us a pot of coffee. Wished we had a fishin' pole. Might catch a trout for supper but guess we'll have to settle for jerky tonight."

"Shouldn't take too long to ride to Mt. Idaho tomorrow, Pete, to get some decent vittles an' a packhorse."

In the morning they were up early riding to Mt. Idaho. They arrived about noon.

"How about we go to an eatin' place first off, Tom?"

"Now that does sound mighty good to me, Pete. I see a saloon up ahead an' an eatin' house right next to it."

They rode up and swung their tired bodies down off the horses, tied them up at the hitching rail and walked in. The people turned and took a good look at these two cowboys. One wearing buckskins and the other dark like an Indian. One man sitting by the front window commented, "Can't say I like the looks of those two men."

"I agree with that. I don't like Injuns," the man with him said.

Tom and Pete heard the comment but ignored it. They sat down and a heavyset woman came over and asked, "What'll you boys have? We have some fine steaks with all the trimmins'."

"That would suit us just fine, ma'am."

When she came back with their meals, Pete asked her, "Where can a man buy a good horse heres about?"

"Down at the other end of town there's a livery stable an' he has horses for sale."

"Thank you, ma'am."

They finished up eating and rode up to the livery stable and inquired of a man inside about buying a horse.

"Yes, sir, boys, I have several good horses for sale. One back there in the back stall is a fine horse, an' reasonable."

"What's your price?"

"He's really worth thirty dollars but I can let you have him for twenty-five."

"Take twenty for him an' you got a sale."

"I'm losin' money at that price, but alright, I'll let you have him for twenty."

Pete counted out twenty and handed it to the man. "We'll be needin' a packsaddle also. Would you know where we could purchase one?"

"Yes, at the mercantile halfway between here and the saloon."

They mounted up, leading the packhorse, a bay gelding, and rode up to the mercantile where they bought a packsaddle and a few staples.

"Tom, let's get to movin'. I don't feel comfortable around here. Don't know if they have a telegraph or not. If they do, they might have got the word on us an' are on the lookout."

"I have that same feelin'. Let's put some distance from this place."

With their packsaddle loaded with a few staples, leading the bay, they headed for the Clearwater. A few hours later they were riding down a trail from the top of the plateau and were in thick timber until they reached the river.

"Pete, I see a spot up the river there amongst the cottonwoods where we can make camp, an' I believe we would be able to see anyone approaching"

"Looks good to me, Tom. Let's get these horses unsaddled and unload the packhorse. I bought some fishhooks an' some line. We can cut us a willow pole an' do some fishin'. Maybe have trout for supper."

"Let's get our camp set up and go fishin', Pete. Trout sounds mighty good for supper."

They unloaded the packhorse, made a little corral for the horses, went down to the riverbank and found some willows. They cut a couple of nice long limber willows, tied a little line on the end with a baited fishing hook, and set out to fish. Pete had gone a short distance downstream.

A short time later he heard Tom holler, "Pete, I just caught a nice size rainbow. One more like this an' we'll have enough for supper."

Pete yelled back, "Just hang on an' I'll catch something that'll make yours look like a minnow." Pete did catch one but it wasn't anything to brag about. They kept fishing but no more bites. Tom had already returned to camp when Pete showed up with his ten-inch trout. Tom's fish must have been at least eighteen inches long. "You should have thrown that minnow back," Tom laughed.

"Let's get a fire goin' and eat," Pete grumbled.

CHAPTER 12—SHERIFF AND POSSE

The posse rode into Council. The first place McCrea went to was the saloon, just to get information.

"You boys wait here an' I'll inquire as to whether anyone has seen our escapers."

"A drink would go down right easy now, Sheriff," Hank Baldwin, one of the posse members, suggested.

One of the other posse members named Jarrod was getting tired of all this fast riding and told the sheriff, "Judd, can't see why we can't let up a little in this pursuit, have a drink or two an' let our bodies rest. I've got blisters on my backsides."

"We don't have time for lyin' around town drinkin'. You can either stay here or just tough it out, Jarrod. I want these men so we can't let up one mite. We can buy a bottle an' have a drink when we set up camp. We'll find out how long ago they were here an' get back on their trail," replied Judd.

"You know, Floyd, I just wonder if there is more to all this hard ridin' than what the sheriff tells us. He's surely obsessed with catchin' these men," Jarrod whispered.

"I agree with you. There's something he's not tellin' us or maybe doesn't want us to know."

Judd swung his six-foot-four frame out of the saddle and walked into the saloon and to the bar.

The barkeep came over and asked him, "What'll you have?"

"Nothin' except I'll take a bottle with me when I leave. Have you seen two men come through here? One was a half-breed an' the other was wearin' buckskins. I'm the sheriff from Silver City an' they're wanted for murder."

"No, an' we don't serve half-breeds. Might ask up at the mercantile or a good source of information would be those two old men sittin' out front. They spend a goodly amount of time just sittin' there smokin', chewin', spittin', whittlin' an' talkin' 'bout anything there is to talk about."

"Much obliged. I'll talk to 'em."

Judd left the bar and found the two men sitting on an old bench just like the barkeep said. He walked up to them and asked, "Old timer, have you seen two men ride through here an' maybe looked like they was in a hurry?"

"What was that, young feller?" he asked.

Judd repeated what he just said.

The other old man spoke up. "I do believe there were two went who through yesterday. Don't remember what time except they were headin' north an' didn't seem to be in a rush."

"Are you sure about that, Henry? You know your eyesight ain't in the finest shape since you got kicked in the head by that mule of you'rn."

"You weren't here yesterday, Caleb, so how would you know?"

They were still arguing as Judd left and joined the posse.

"Boys, it doesn't appear they stopped here. Still ridin' north. They maybe still most of a day ahead of us. I think we're getting' closer. We'll ride to Mt. Idaho before we stop for the night. With fresh mounts we could close on 'em faster because I don't believe they've changed horses since they left," the sheriff told them.

The sheriff and posse rode hard. Just as the sun was going down, they entered Mt. Idaho.

Tracker Dan Wilkerson had rode on ahead looking for tracks. Returning, he reined up by the sheriff. "Sheriff, there're so many tracks, can't tell if any are Tom's an' Pete's. Nowhere else they could really go, so I'd wager they went into Mt. Idaho an' bought supplies. They have to eat."

"I'd wager you're right, Dan. We'll check the mercantile an' see if they bought any staples. Hank, you an' Floyd check out the livery stable and see if they've done some business there. Jarrod, check out the other saloon. See if they was in there."

Judd and Dan rode up to the mercantile, dismounted and walked in. As they entered the store, on the left was bacon, hardtack, eggs and other staples. On the other side the smell in the air was the odor of fresh leather goods. In the back was a cast iron stove, a bench and a spittoon. A skinny old man wearing spectacles and suspenders, smoking a corncob pipe, approached them and asked, "Can I help you, cowboys?"

"You surely can. Did you see two men yesterday, one dark like a Indian an' the other wearin' buckskins?"

"Sure have. Are you lawmen?"

"I'm the sheriff from Silver City an' we've been on the trail of these two for quite a spell."

"Well, Sheriff, as I recollect, they were here yesterday, bought supplies includin' a packsaddle."

"What way were they headed?"

"Didn't pay much mind, but believe they rode east toward the stable. You might inquire there."

"We'll do that."

They walked out, mounted their horses and headed east. Hank and Floyd were riding toward them and reined up next to them. "Sheriff, they were at the stable, bought a packhorse an' he noticed when they left they were headed in the direction of the Clearwater River."

"Let's ride over to the stable an' see if we can acquire fresh horses," Judd told them.

Judd told the stable man, "I'm Sheriff Judd McCrea from Silver City and we're on the trail of an escaped killer an' his partner. They bought a horse from you."

"Yes, I recollect 'em. They were in need of a packhorse an' I sold 'em one. Didn't seem like murderers to me."

"Well they are, an' we intend to catch 'em. We've been ridin' our horses fairly hard an' need fresh horses. I have a warrant. Can you supply us? We need seven."

"Yes, I believe I can. I'll have to do business with hard cash, an' extra because mine are in fine shape where yours is none too good. I think ten dollars a horse would be a fair trade. That'd come to seventy dollars."

"You're on the high side but we'll take 'em," replied Judd. "Let's get our saddles changed. Who am I doin' business with?"

"Name's John Ambrose an' I'm the owner of the livery barn. It's been a pleasure dealin' with you, Sheriff."

The posse changed horses and rode out of town toward the Clearwater River.

"We'll ride hard till dark an' make camp. I want to close the distance as much as we can."

They rode another ten miles before stopping for the night.

"Looks like a good place to set up camp just up yonder," the tracker said.

I have to catch these two men. If it weren't for the men with me, I'd see that Tom an' Pete didn't make it back to Silver City. Someone could blow the whistle on the rustling an' I could hang. I have to catch them an' soon. Don't know what those men at the Bar-0-1 might be up to, Judd thought.

They were up before dawn and headed down the plateau towards the Clearwater. They had been in the saddle an hour or so when Dan came back from his scouting ahead and announced, "I do believe we're getting' close, Sheriff. I found a trail with three sets of tracks, all shod. By the horse dropping's I would wager they're not too far ahead."

"You keep on that trail, Dan. Don't get too close an' alert 'em. We need to catch 'em off guard. I'm sure they won't give up without a fight."

"Stay on this trail, Sheriff, an' I'll report back when I have something."

Dan disappeared into the timber an' the posse picked up the pace, some hoping this long trip would be over soon.

The cook was having some serious thoughts. "I'm getting' a little nervous now that we are getting' close to a shoot-out. I'm not lookin' forward to bein' shot at," Basset muttered to himself.

"I believe I hear the river, boys. Be on the alert an' keep the horses as quiet as possible. The river will muffle the sound of our horses some," Judd told them.

They rode another mile or two when Hank said, "I see a rider coming up the trail."

"Hold up. It might be Dan," replied the sheriff.

It was. He reined up next to McCrea. "I spotted a camp an' two men. Couldn't be sure who they were but I believe it's them. Three horses tied up among the cottonwood trees."

"That's good news, Dan. I want to surround 'em before they know it an' get the drop on 'em. Like to capture 'em alive if possible.

"Dan, you an' Hank come with me. Jarrod, you an' Floyd go downstream an' get in position so they can't escape that way. Will, you stay here on the trail an' keep a sharp eye out."

"That sure sounds good to me. Ain't hankerin' to be down there with the shootin'."

The posse moved into position, surrounding the camp.

"Dan, I want to move a little closer an' see who has that camp," the sheriff said.

The three of them eased themselves down between large boulders just up from the river. The sheriff motioned for them to be quiet.

Judd had a deep feeling of contentment as he spotted Tom and Pete. This chase was going to be over at last. The horses in Tom and Pete's camp were snorting and shifting around in their rope corral.

"Did you hear that, Pete? Somethin' or someone is up there in the timber. I don't like this. Better get behind those rocks 'til we find out what's disturbin' the horses."

"Let's move, Tom. Grab my rifle there by you."

Before they could get to the safety of the rocks, there was a yell from up above them.

"This is Sheriff McCrea. You boys throw down your guns. This time you're surrounded an' outgunned. If you try a shoot-out I guarantee you won't come out alive. You best give up."

"Don't believe we have a chance, Pete. Right now I wish Alokut would show up with his braves."

"Alright, Tom. Guess you're right, but it's a long way back to Silver City. Maybe Alokut will run into us on the way back. As far as I can see he's our only hope. We should have rode to the Wallowas with him."

The sheriff yelled, "What's it goin' to be, Tom?"

"Alright, Sheriff, we give up. We're comin' out in the open."

Tom and Pete came out where the posse could see them and laid their guns down. The sheriff and his posse moved down and collected the firearms.

"It's late so I reckon we'll stay here the night an' head out in the mornin'. Tie 'em up good. I don't intend to lose 'em this time," Judd told them.

A deputy asked the cook, "How's about cookin' us up somethin' good tonight? Sort of a celebration so to speak."

"I'm afraid it'll only be beans an' some bacon. Reckon I could whip up some biscuits too if I was a mind to."

"You boys take turn keepin' night watch on these two men. They're slick," the sheriff instructed.

"Hey, Sheriff, have you told your deputies about your little sideline business you an' the judge have goin'?" Tom asked.

"What's he talkin' about, Judd? You wouldn't be doin' somethin' illegal now, would you?" Dan asked.

"Don't listen to 'em. They'll say anything to save their necks."

"Tell 'em about Ben Ross an' when I caught him with a bunch of rustled beef," replied Pete.

"Pete, I'm not goin' to keep jawin' about this. Ben was in court an' he cleared himself of any wrongdoin'. You boys know that since I reckon most of you were there at the trial."

"I'd wager you're right, Judd. I was there," Hank Baldwin said.

"Well it'll all come out someday an' maybe after I'm gone, but this is not over. Not by a jug full," commented Tom.

"If you an' Pete don't shut your mouths, I'll have to gag you," Judd said.

"You know, boys, we ought to stay here tomorrow an' do a little fishin'. Tom an' Pete have willows all cut. Rest up some afore we head back; we've got a long ways to travel. I'm sure our outlaws won't mind stickin' around with us since they're not goin' anywhere. Ain't that right, Tom?" McCrea commented.

"That sounds like a right smart idea. Let my backside heal some," replied the deputy with saddle sores.

"Sounds good to me too, McCrea. Maybe you'll fall in an' drown. It would be no loss," Tom commented.

"You're beginnin' to irritate me."

"Grubs ready, boys. Come an' get it," the cook announced.

"How you goin' feed the prisoners, Sheriff?" the tracker asked.

"I feel like not feedin 'em at all but we have to keep 'em alive 'til we reach Silver City. Loosen their hands but keep a watch on 'em," Judd ordered.

"You're a fine cook, Basset. Not bad for a deputy," replied Pete.

"I must say this is a right pleasin' feelin' to have these two in custody. We can sit back, relax and enjoy the night air. Do a little fishin' tomorrow and just rest up afore we head back," Judd remarked.

"Who's takin' the first watch?" Dan asked.

"One of you deputies take the first watch till midnight, another can spell him to four or so an' then Jarrod can take it 'til we all roust out in the mornin'. Make sure they're tied good," Judd said.

They were all in their bedrolls and asleep except for their guard. About eleven Hank dozed off and Tom whispered to Pete, "Do you reckon there might be a chance we'll meet Alokut an' his band on our way back, an' if we do, you think he'll rescue us or not get involved?"

"Can't say. Don't know if we have much of a chance to even see him. We better be thinkin' on other ways to escape."

Daylight brought some stirring in camp. The cook was up fixing some vittles and started waking up the camp, fixing a fire and banging around.

The tracker spoke up, "Hey, can't you make a little less noise? A man can't get any rest with you makin' such a commotion."

"Sorry about that, Dan, but you know these men, when they want something to eat, they want it now! Besides, if the sheriff or anyone is goin' try his hand at fishin', early morning's the time to do it. If someone would be lucky an' catch a few, I would cook 'em up for breakfast. Well lookee there, I see Judd's arousin'."

"You are one noisy cook, Will; I was enjoyin' my sleep 'til you woke me."

"Sorry, Sheriff, but I figured you might want to try fishin'. A few trout would go good for mornin' chuck, wouldn't you say?"

Pete and Tom were awake and Tom told their guard, "We need to go in the woods an' talk to Mother Nature."

"Alright, wait 'til I get one of the other boys to watch Pete."

"I need to do the same thing," replied Pete.

"You can wait 'til Tom is through. Sheriff wants us to keep a close eye on the two of you. One of you men come over here an' watch Pete while I take Tom out in the woods."

After Tom and Pete had finished they were tied back up. There wasn't anyone close to them and Tom whispered, "Did you notice how our guard sleeps? I believe a gun could be fired off beside him an' he wouldn't wake up. Last night I was workin' with these ropes on my wrists an' if they don't tie them any tighter, I just might be able to get out of 'em. If we could get loose we could try to sneak out, grab our horses an' escape."

"Don't know, Tom. They'd all have to sleep sound, but maybe if we could get loose, grab our guards gun an' we'd be in control."

"If we get the same man guardin' us tonight, I think I can get my hands loose. I asked our guard if he could loosen the ropes on my hands just a mite. Told him the ropes was cuttin' into my wrist so he did. I would wager he didn't think we would have a chance for any escape. I noticed the one guard likes his whiskey and has been drinkin' quite a bit in the evenin'. That's probably why he sleeps so sound. Maybe tonight they'll be celebratin' some since they have us in custody."

"Sounds good, Tom. Let's be ready."

"Will, we have a string of fish for you to cook this mornin'. Surely would be fine with some of those biscuits of yourn. Don't know if we have enough for our prisoners though. They can settle for beans," the sheriff said.

"I reckon I can whip up some biscuits. Are we goin' to head back in the mornin', Judd?" Will asked.

"I reckon so. I'm anxious to get back to Silver City with these outlaws and into a real bed. We'll rest up here today, do a little more fishin'. Might have more trout for tonight."

After morning chuck, a couple of the deputies walked down to the river to try their luck. They came back to camp with a few trout.

Later on that afternoon the cook whipped up some biscuits, fried the fish, and with some beans had their supper.

They were all lying around having a smoke when the sheriff announced, "Boys, I believe this whole trip calls for a bottle. Will, break out those two bottles in the pack boxes. I reckon we deserve a few drinks this evenin'. What'd you cowboys think?"

"That surely does sound right fittin' to us," they remarked.

One thing for certain, their guard Jarrod liked his whiskey. They were passing the bottle around and Tom asked, "How about sharin', Sheriff?"

"Can't do that, Tom, bein's you're an Injun. Gainst the law, and I reckon you've got some Injun in you too, Pete. Injuns always get mean an' rowdy an' we can't abide that."

"Don't think you're any too funny. Maybe someday you'll get your comeuppance," replied Pete.

The sun was sinking in the west and the remaining light was streaming through the poplar and pine trees along the bank of the river, casting shadows across the camp. The posse was consuming the whiskey and generally having a good time and getting a little noisy. They were sitting around the campfire passing the two bottles around. The whiskey was beginning to loosen some tongues.

"Judd, you want to tell us more about this rustlin' you were accused of?" the tracker asked.

"Ain't nothin' to say 'cause they're liars. Besides, if I was makin' a little money on the side, what's the matter with that? I'm sure anyone of you boys would do the same. We all enjoy money an' good whiskey." The firewater was loosening Judd's tongue a little.

"It just seems as you were in such an' all fired hurry to catch 'em. Never seen you go after anyone this hard before."

"Sheriff, you can be honest with us," commented one of the posse members.

"Nothin' to be honest about. I reckon we should drop the subject an' get some shuteye. It's a long way back to Silver City an' accordin' to my pocket watch it's nigh onto midnight," Judd told them. He was returning to his senses and it was time to keep his mouth shut.

"Why don't you tell 'em the truth, Sheriff, about your rustlin' operation you an' Judge Potter have goin'?" Tom spoke up.

"If you don't shut your mouth, I'll have to gag you. You don't know what you're talkin' about," replied the sheriff.

The whole crew was in their bedrolls snoring except Tom and Pete who were just waiting to see how sound they would sleep. Just as they figured, the guard that had been slugging the booze down wasn't doing a good job guarding. It was about two in the morning and the red glow of the campfire still gave out some light. Tom motioned to Pete. He was loose. He had to be very quiet and get the ropes off his feet. He crawled over where the guard was sitting against a tree and grabbed the rifle next to him.

The guard was asleep and snoring. He crawled back over to Pete, loosened his hands and Pete removed the ropes from his legs.

"Time to wake our deputies up, Pete." At that time Tom yelled, "Hey, boys, it's time to roust out of those bedrolls."

Judd woke rubbing his eyes, not realizing his prisoners were loose. "Who the hell is wakin' me at this hour? It's still dark."

Then he saw Tom standing over him. "How in tarnation did you get loose?" He yelled at the ones who were assigned to guard the prisoners, "How did they manage to get out of those ropes? You were supposed to check an' make sure they were tied proper."

"They were, Sheriff," replied a deputy as he was trying to get himself awake.

Pete went around gathering up guns. "What we goin' to do with 'em?" asked Pete. "Think we ought to kill 'em all?"

"No, some of 'em have families an' we don't want to be like the sheriff. If it hadn't been for his deputies he would have killed us."

"That ain't so, Tom. I would have taken you both back an' you would have had a fair trial."

"Don't rightly believe so," remarked Pete.

"Let's quit this palavering an' decide what we're goin' to do with 'em, Pete. I suggest we put 'em afoot. Take their horses except leave 'em with the packhorse they brung. Take 'em quite a spell to walk back to Mt. Idaho."

"Sounds like a right fine idea, Tom."

"Alright, men, you heard. Take your packhorse an' head out. Sorry we can't let you have any guns. Wouldn't be fittin' now would it?" replied Pete.

"You'll be mighty sorry for this, Tom, I'll guarantee you that. I'll hunt you down an' I won't show you any mercy," the sheriff said.

"It's not going to happen, Judd, so I suggest you fellas get to walkin'. You've quite a hike ahead of you," Tom told them.

The sheriff and deputies, leading their packhorse, headed up through the timber toward Mt. Idaho. Tom and Pete put all the guns except the rifles on their packhorse. The rifles were kept in the scabbards on the posse's horses.

"I wonder how long it'll take 'em to reach town," Tom said to Pete.

"I would wager all of two days."

"I bet Judd is fit to be tied," remarked Tom.

"Let's ride on over the mountains to Montana, Tom. Be smart to put some distance between the posse an' us because Judd's no fool. I'd expect him to acquire more horses an' come after us an' maybe with a bigger posse if he can recruit any."

Tom and Pete headed out with their string of nine horses, riding the Lolo Trail, a steep climb through large rock and pine timber following the Clearwater to the top of the Bitterroot Mountains.

"We need to get rid of these extra saddles an' horses. I'd guess we could sell them at a tradin' post, no questions asked. I know of one over in the Bitterroot valley. Might be we could hole up somewhere around there, wait for Alokut an' his band," Pete said.

"I hope Judd's feet are gettin' sore by now. I would wager he's madder than a wet hen," remarked Tom.

"I reckon we'll be safe enough to make camp at the pass. It'll be a spell before the sheriff an' his deputies will be able to ride out after us," Pete said.

"He has no jurisdiction in Montana. Do you reckon he'll come after us anyway?" replied Tom.

"It would be my guess, Tom, as he's a determined man an' doesn't like to have been made a fool of. I'd wager he'd try to get the US Cavalry involved. I see a good place to rest for the night up yonder among those pines an' large rocks that would give us good protection should anyone try to attack us. In the mornin' we can ride to the tradin' post."

They made camp at the summit of the Bitterroots at the headwaters of the Clearwater.

"I believe it's safe to have a small fire so we can have coffee an' grub, don't you reckon, Pete?"

"Don't see why we can't. I'm sure McCrea is quite a distance behind us."

"Maybe in time we can go back to Silver City an' prove my innocence."

"Don't know, Tom. Before that ever happens, I would venture to say we'd have to kill the sheriff. He's not goin' to give up until he gets rid of us. I wonder if the boys at the Bar-O-1 have managed to steal back the cattle."

"If they have, I'd wager Judge Potter is madder than a wet hen," replied Tom.

"Let's get in our bedrolls an' get up early. Don't want to be dilly-dallying around here long. It would be my guess that McCrea is hot on our trail," Pete told him.

Next morning they were riding down the Montana side of the Bitterroots.

"I see the valley now, Tom. Shouldn't be long before we reach the tradin' post."

They had come down out of the timber to enter expanses of grassland. This was cattle and buffalo country. They traveled on a well-used trail, the same one used by the Nez Perce for generations. After riding steady for several hours, in the early afternoon they spotted the trading post. There were several Indian ponies tied up out front.

"I see he has a pole corral there on the side of the post. Let's put our horses in, Pete, an' go in an' talk to the owner."

Tom dismounted, opened the gate and Pete led the string in, tying the horses up. Didn't want them rolling with their saddles on. They walked into the post and the owner was dealing with some Indians. There were piles of blankets on one side and saddles and leather goods on the other side. Behind him on shelves were beans, flour, sugar, salt, and bottles of whiskey. They overheard him say, "No whiskey to you Injuns."

He looked up and saw Pete and Tom. He recognized Pete. "I'd know you anywhere, Pete, with those buckskins. Don't you ever take them off?" He laughed.

"I see you haven't changed either. Just as ornery as ever."

"What are you doin' in these parts, Pete, an' who's the Injun you have with you?"

"Caleb, we run into a passel of trouble down Silver City way an' are on the run from a sheriff from Silver City by the name of Judd McCrea."

"I've heard of him, an' they're not very good reports."

"This my friend Tom an' he's wanted for shootin' a man in self-defense. They had us in custody but we broke free down on the Clearwater. We took their horses, saddles an' guns. We'd like to sell 'em to you, if you have a mind to buy at a reasonable price."

"Let's go take a look at 'em. I just might be able to unload the horses an' saddles to these Injuns here."

They walked out to the corral and the post owner remarked, “I’ll talk to the Injuns an’ see what we can do. You boys wait here.”

It was quite awhile before he returned, but when he showed up he told them, “If your price is not too high, the Injuns an’ I agreed on a price. I need to get rid of ’em today. Wouldn’t want the sheriff showin’ up an’ I have the horses, saddles and other gear. I reckon I’ll hide the guns. Don’t want the Injuns havin’ ’em.”

Tom, Pete and the trading post owner agreed on the price including rifles and saddles. The Indians rode off leading the string.

“I never thought I’d be this dishonest, Pete, but the sheriff put us in this condition. Now we’ll have a charge of horse stealin’ also.”

“Yes, and that’s a hangin’ offense, but if we could prove the judge and sheriff were involved in rustlin’, I believe they’d let us off, Tom.”

“We best be ridin’ out of here, Pete.”

“Yep, we need to hide out somewhere an’ wait for Alokut an’ his band. With the Indians we’d be safe unless Judd gets the cavalry after us too. Maybe we can head north or we could double back an’ head back to Idaho. That would confuse the posse maybe—just maybe. I suggest we ride back to the Lolo Trail an’ see if we can find the Nez Perce,” Pete said.

They rode in the direction of the trail hoping they would run into Alokut.

Chapter 13—THE LONG WALK

"Jarrod, if I had a gun I would shoot you right here for lettin' Tom get the drop on you," Judd told the deputy.

"It would have happened to you if you'd have been in my spot. Didn't see you sleepin' with one eye open."

"Oh shut up," the sheriff replied.

"Don't know about you fellas but walkin' in these boots wasn't meant to be," the tracker commented.

"How long you expect it'll take to reach Mt. Idaho, Dan?" the sheriff asked

"Dunno. We passed one ranch on the way here. Maybe we can get fresh mounts there."

"If we can get horses an' guns, we can get back on the trail of the outlaws," replied Judd.

"Not me. I'm ridin' for home soon as we get to town. If we was to catch up with Tom an' Pete again, there'll be shootin' for sure an' you ain't payin' enough to get shot or killed, Sheriff," a deputy said.

"That goes for me too," another replied.

"Maybe in Mt. Idaho I can find men with grit that'd ride with me. I don't intend for these men to get away a second time. Perhaps get the army involved," Judd said. "It's gettin' dark an' I think it best we hole up here for the night. My feet are killin' me."

"We should pass that ranch sometime in the mornin'," Dan told them.

"I'll say one thing. We're lucky they left us with our packhorse an' supplies," commented Deputy Baldwin.

The cook got a fire going and was whipping up some grub. After they ate they slid into their bedrolls and were instantly asleep. They were tired from the walking. In the morning the cook was the first one up. He got a fire started and a pot of coffee brewing.

The sheriff announced after the coffee they would head for the ranch. "I would wager we can get us a decent meal at the ranch."

They packed up the horse and with sore feet were walking west.

"My feet are about to give up. Don't know how much longer I can take this," the deputy responsible for Tom and Pete's escape said.

The sheriff turned around and said, "Quit your bellyachin'. Because of you is why we're here in the first place. When we get to town, you can head home. I don't want you in my posse."

They came to a fork in the road. There was a sign pointing towards the ranch. A mile down the road the ranch house could be spotted among a grove of pine trees. One side of the road was a small, fast-moving stream with thick willows and poplars on the side. Beyond the poplars were large grass meadows. They all stopped, took their boots off and soaked their tired feet in the cool water for a spell before continuing.

"Let's get to movin'," the sheriff told them. "Don't know how I got hooked up with a bunch like this."

When they reached the house it appeared deserted.

"I see a note on the door," replied a deputy.

Judd pulled it off and read it. "Doesn't look like we're goin' to get any horses here. It says because the Indians are starting to stir up trouble around here, they have left until all the trouble is over. Says to help ourselves to whatever we need. There's home-canned food in the cellar behind the house and a little bacon in the smokehouse."

"I say we rest up for a spell, maybe a day. My feet are sore an' I reckon yours are too," the tracker said.

"I'd wager you're right. It's goin' take a little longer to catch those outlaws. Best we spend the night here an' have somethin' to eat. Let's go on into the house. Be a sight more comfortable, an' safer too." Judd told them.

"If one of you boys will bring in some wood, I'll cook us up some vittles," the cook said.

It was a tired bunch of men and it didn't take them long to get some shuteye. Next morning after the cook fixed them something they started walking again. The deputy, who went to sleep on guard duty and was causing this walk to happen, made the comment, "I'm too tired to go on. Why can't we rest up here for another day, Sheriff?"

"Tell you what. As far as I'm concerned you can stay here forever. Maybe the Indians will come by an' put you out of your misery. Sure'd make me no never mind."

He wasn't about to be left behind, so with a lot of grunting and groaning he joined the rest on their walk.

They had been walking for several hours when in the distance they could see a cloud of dust. They couldn't make out what it was.

"We'd better get off this road an' hide in the brush 'til we see who it is. Might be Indians," the sheriff said.

They all scrambled into the thicket, concealing themselves, and waited.

"Surely hope it's not Injuns since we don't have guns," commented the tracker.

"Keep your voices down," the sheriff told them.

The riders appeared to be riding in formation.

"It's the cavalry. What a relief," the tracker said.

They led their packhorse out onto the road and waited for the troops to arrive.

When the troops arrived the officer in charge motioned for his command to rein up. He noticed the badge on Judd's shirt. "I see you're a lawman. What are you men doin' out here without no mounts?"

"Captain, who am I addressin'?" Judd asked.

"I'm Captain Perry an' we're on a routine patrol. The Nez Perce are actin' up some. How come you to be afoot, sheriff?"

"We were on a chase after some outlaws; captured 'em down on the Clearwater. They managed to get loose, grab a gun an' get the drop on us. Tryin' to get to Mt. Idaho, get fresh mounts and go after the outlaws. One is a half breed an' I'm thinkin' maybe they've joined up with the Indians."

"Hard story to swallow, Sheriff, when there's six of you. You all must have been liquored up to let that happen."

The sheriff didn't want to say that was the problem.

"We'd be mighty grateful if one of your men could ride into town an' bring back some horses."

"Sorry, Sheriff. Can't spare a man. I need everyone. It's only about fifteen miles into town. You should make it by evenin'. We have to be on our way. Those men are probably in Montana by now. If we run into 'em we'll detain 'em an' bring 'em back to Mt. Idaho when we return in four or five days."

"Thank you, Captain. I reckon we'll be on our way."

With a salute the captain and his troop rode out of sight and Judd and his deputies were again plodding toward town. The deputies were tired and stretched out far between each other. Judd and the tracker were in the lead. The sheriff was mad and determined. He hollered back at his men, "You men best get up here closer! Not that I care, but strung out like this Indians could pick you off one by one!"

"Well hold up, Sheriff, so we can catch up. Our feet are killin' us an' we can't walk as fast as you. The way my feet feel I couldn't care one whit about any Indians. Might put me out of my misery," one commented.

"All right, we'll stop an' rest," replied the sheriff.

After a rest they resumed their walk towards town. By late evening they arrived in town. The first place they went to was the bar. All six tired men leaned up against the bar and the bartender asked, "What'll you boys have?"

"Bring us a cool beer."

"We'll drink this beer an' go to the sheriff's office. See if we can get some men to go with us," the sheriff commented.

Two of his deputies spoke up, "You can go after 'em all you want. We're goin' home." The other three said they would stay and go with him.

The two deputies going home walked to the livery stable to see about horses and McCrea and the other three went to the local sheriff's office. They entered the office where a short, fat man sat behind a desk, his feet on the desk. He was leaning back against the wall sound asleep. McCrea kicked the desk. The man jumped and almost fell off his chair.

"Hey, what's the idea startlin' me like that? What'd you want? Oh, I see you're a lawman. What can I do for you?"

"I'm the sheriff from Silver City. We need horses an' some men with grit to help us recapture two outlaws who escaped from our custody."

"I'm right sorry about that, Sheriff, but I'm the only law in town. As you see, I can't go with you an' leave this town defenseless. You might try the local bar for extra men but I doubt you'll find any willin' to leave their families an' traipse all over the country since the Injuns are actin' up some. As far as findin' horses, you might try the livery stable. He most always has a few."

Judd thanked him and they left. He couldn't help thinking, *what did he mean leave the town defenseless? With him in office it already is.*

They walked into the livery barn and Judd asked the owner, "We need four horses with saddles an' I have a warrant that'll pay for 'em."

"I don't have much right now except two mules an' that sorrel work horse back there in the back stalls. I can let you have 'em on your warrant. Two men came in a short time ago an' bought the only good horses I had left. I'm somewhat short on saddles too, but I reckon I can fix you up with somethin'."

"Not exactly what I had in mind to ride but I'm anxious to get on the trail. We'll settle for 'em," Judd told him. "You boys saddle up these crow baits so we can get back on the trail. I'll ride the packhorse as I hate mules, an' you boys take what's left. Maybe later we can trade for somethin' better. We'll ride to the mercantile an' buy a few staples. We won't be needin' the pack-saddle. We'll take the two mules an' one plow horse."

They bought some needed grub, put it in their saddlebags, and were riding back in the direction where they last saw Tom and Pete at the Clearwater River. The sheriff was unable to enlist any men from town to join the posse.

"We're getting' a late start so I reckon we'll have to spend a night afore we get there. Do you think you can find their trail again, Dan?"

"I reckon I can, Sheriff, since it hasn't rained yet."

Next morning they were up early and riding to where Tom and Pete had overpowered them.

One of the deputies remarked, "This mule is mighty easy ridin'. Just not much to look at an' if we was chased by Indians I'd wager they'd catch us easy."

"Well, I'll tell you this old plow horse is not very comfortable. I'll be mighty grateful when we get someplace where we can trade 'em off," a deputy remarked.

"Don't reckon we'll find a place to do any tradin' 'til we get to Montana," the sheriff said.

They arrived at the camp where Tom and Pete escaped, crossed the river and headed up the Lolo Trail.

"I see many horse tracks an' one hoof print I believe is my horse because of an oddshaped front shoe. This is the logical way for them to ride, I would say," Dan Wilkerson commented.

The tracker rode on ahead. He had stopped and was looking back down the trail waiting for the posse to arrive. He motioned and pointed over to some large rocks and timber. When they arrived he told the sheriff, "They camped here an' the tracks lead out down the mountain. I suggest we stay here for the night."

"All right, we'll do that since it's gettin' late. Unsaddle your horses an' tie 'em up over there among the pines," the sheriff told them.

"Are you goin' get the Montana authorities involved? You know you don't have a legal right in this state," one of the deputies remarked.

"I don't reckon I will unless they happen to be close. I intend to capture these two an' take 'em back to Silver City, dead or alive.

Doesn't matter which," the sheriff replied. "It's been twelve days since we left. I don't want to be all summer after 'em. We'll just have to ride harder."

In the morning they headed down the mountain following a trail that led to the valley below.

"It appears by the tracks they're ridin' that way. This is a heavy traveled trail. I expect we'll find a settlement afore long," the tracker commented.

"I see smoke yonder 'bout a mile," McCrea said.

"Hold up, Sheriff. I want to take a gander at these tracks."

The tracker dismounted and looked over a passel of tracks. Down on his haunches, he turned and looked up at Judd. "These are their tracks for sure. I'd recognize that crooked shoe of my horse anywhere. I think we might be gettin' close. These look real fresh."

Dan mounted up and they rode on. The smoke they had seen earlier was close enough to make out a building and some corrals. "Looks like a tradin' post, Judd. Don't see any horses around except two in back."

The posse reined up in front of the trading post, dismounted and walked into the building. A gray bearded man behind a counter piled high with fur pelts greeted them.

"Hello, cowboys, name's Caleb; what can I do for you? I've got just about anything you might be needin', even whiskey if you happen to be on the thirsty side."

"Right off I want to know if two riders came through here with eight saddled horses an' one packhorse recently," the sheriff said.

"Can't say there has been, Sheriff. Some Injuns were here yesterday is all."

The tracker walked in and overheard what he said. "He's lyin', Judd.; I checked the corral and found the tracks of my horse."

"All right, old man, I'm not goin' to fool with you. Tell me the truth or I'll beat it out of you," Judd told him.

"Like I told you, no one but Injuns have been here of late," he replied.

"Take him outside an' tie him to that tree. He'll talk or I'll flail the meat off his back."

Two of the deputies dragged the old man out and tied him to an oak tree in front. Judd pulled his belt off and said, "Old man, this is your last chance. Talk.

"Rip his shirt off. I want to see bare hide."

Deputy Baldwin said, "Judd, I don't like this. I'm not into beatin' an old man. Next thing it will be some old woman or young boy."

"I'll tell you what, Deputy, if you don't shut up I'll give you the same, an' that goes for any of the rest of you. Now stand back."

He hit the old man several times across the back but he refused to talk. Judd hit him a few more times and he slumped over.

"I think you killed him," the deputy that was against the beating said.

"He's not dead. Untie him an' throw some water in his face. Maybe that'll arouse him an' he'll be ready to tell me something," Judd told him.

The water revived him and he agreed to tell what he knew.

"They rode east towards the Rockies an' they sold all the horses except the ones they was ridin' an' a packhorse to some Pend d' Oreille Injuns that were here." He was lying but he wasn't about to tell this sheriff the truth. He didn't want to die and this man was capable of killing.

"If you're tellin' me a lie, I'll come back an' burn your business to the ground," Judd promised him. "What direction did the Injuns ride, an' where can we find horses? One of you boys search his place an' see if you can find any guns."

"The Injuns rode north towards Canada an' there is a large ranch east in the direction you'll be goin'. They run a lot of horses."

A deputy came out with a bunch of rifles and some pistols.

"These are our guns, Sheriff. He had them hid."

"I ought to shoot him now an' maybe I will when we come back through," replied Judd. "Mount up. I don't want to waste any more time around here. I want some good horses an' we need saddles."

"We're goin' to be in a heap of trouble if the cavalry or a US marshal comes by here. I think we ought to turn around, forget about

Tom an' Pete. We've been gone 'bout twelve days now an' we ain't any better off than when we started," one of the deputies commented.

"We're goin' on whether you like it or not," McCrea told him.

"I don't see any tracks goin' this way," the tracker said.

"We need horses. After we acquire 'em we'll double back an' see if we can locate their trail again," the sheriff told him.

The posse rode east toward the ranch, hoping to find horses. They had ridden close to ten miles, where nestled down in a small valley surrounded by grassy hills, they saw the ranch. They rode up to the front of a large log house and were met by a tall older man with a gray handlebar mustache.

"What can I do for you, gents? From the looks of what you're ridin' I'd be willin' to wager you've come to see me about horses, an' that's somethin' I do have."

"That's exactly why we're here. We're lawmen from Idaho after two men that maybe you've seen," Judd told him.

"No, hasn't been a soul through here in two weeks."

"We need three horses an' we'd like to trade these mules an' the sorrel. Also saddles if you have any. I do have a warrant that will guarantee you'll get your money. Whom might I be dealin' with?"

"Name's Jim Grey, the owner of this spread. I don't believe you have any authority in Montana. How can I be sure of my money?"

"I'll tell you, Mr. Grey. You'll have to trust me. We can just take the horses an' I don't see where you could do much about it," replied Judd.

"Don't reckon that'd be very smart of you. I have riders workin' for me an' they're right handy with guns. I'll tell you what I'll do for you. I presume these men have committed a crime an' I believe in upholdin' the law. I will let you have three horses at seventy-five dollars each with the trade of your two mules an' sorrel. I don't have any saddles to spare. I expect a paper guaranteeing my money within thirty days."

"That's robbery," Judd remarked.

"It's either that or you boys can ride out of here on what you rode in on. Makes no never mind to me. Now who might I be doin' business with?"

"I'm Sheriff Judd McCrea from Silver city, Idaho."

"I need proof that you're who you say you are."

Judd pulled out a warrant showing they were after Tom and Pete.

"Well I reckon that'll suit me." He walked down to his barn and brought out his buckskin. "Mount up an' we'll go to the south pasture. My men won't be in 'til this evenin'."

When they arrived, Jim Grey pointed out the horses he would let them have.

"Take those two sorrels an' the bay down by the creek."

They cut them out and drove them back to the ranch house to a corral out in back.

"These are not the best of horse flesh, Mr. Grey."

"With me puttin' my trust in you, you think I'd give you my finest?" he replied.

"You men get those horses saddled up so we can be on our way," Judd told his deputies. "We'll ride northwest an' see if we can pick up their trail again."

Jim Grey smiled as he watched the riders disappear in the distance. "Even if I don't get my money I'll break even with these mules alone. They're fine animals. That sheriff doesn't know the value of mules, especially in the mining country where they need surefooted beasts to carry dynamite and supplies back into the rugged mountains."

CHAPTER 14—THE NEZ PERCE

Tom and Pete made camp on a high hill where they could watch for the Nez Perce.

"We best not have a very big fire. Just large enough to cook some grub. We don't know where the sheriff is," Pete said.

"I have a feelin' he's not too far away. Don't reckon he's forgot us by a long shot. He's not the giv'n up type," remarked Tom. "You know we either have to kill him or prove his rustlin'."

"You're right, Tom, but if we're with the Nez Perce he won't attempt anything unless he has the army involved. We best turn in an' get some sleep, an' we better sleep with one eye open."

In the morning they aroused early and decided to stay where they were, as they had a good view of the valley below and the trail leading down the mountain from Idaho. They hadn't been watching very long when Tom spoke up. "Pete, I see riders comin' down the Lolo an' best I can make out is they're Indians. Hopefully it is Alokut's band."

"They should pass close enough to see who they are, Tom."

They didn't have to wait long before the riders were close enough to see they were Indians.

"Let's ride, Tom."

The horses were already saddled. They mounted up and rode down the hill where they were in sight of the Indians. They stopped and waited. The Nez Perce arrived, led by Alokut. He rode forward to greet them.

"It is good to see you again, my brother. Are you going to go hunt the buffalo with us?"

"We'd like to ride with you, but we're being followed by a posse," Pete said.

"Come with us and you will be safe from them unless the cavalry is after you also. We have not seen any so you will have no trouble while you're with us. Let us be on our way. We will make camp early and ride on east until we locate the buffalo," the chief told them.

There were about a hundred Nez Perce including women, young men, girls and braves. They arrived at a river and set up the tepees. The women began preparing the evening meal. After eating the braves gathered around telling stories of past hunts. Some were exaggerated. Some of the young girls were giggling and looking over at Tom.

One of the girls told another, "He would make you a fine husband. He is handsome and looks very strong."

"He does not interest me," replied the girl named Mal-lit-tay-lay.

Tom was gazing over at the girls and noticed one was very pretty. He couldn't hear what they were saying but saw they were looking at him. Pete was talking to Alokut and some other braves. He motioned for Tom to come over.

"Tom, I have mentioned to the chief that you need a wife an' he said that can be arranged."

Through that dark skin of his they could see him blushing. "I don't need a wife right now, Pete."

"I think you'd be wise to marry one of the Nez Perce girls an' stay with the tribe instead of goin' back to Oregon. The chief is going to introduce you to some young maidens that need a husband."

Tom could tell Pete was enjoying this. Later that evening Alokut came over to where Tom was and told him, "Come with me. I will show you some young girls that would make you a fine wife."

Tom wanted to tell him forget it, as he wasn't too interested. They walked over where all the women were and they all gathered around to see what the chief was going to say. Alokut motioned to a girl to come over. He told Tom her name was Lo-oh-hee. Tom noticed she was pretty but he couldn't keep his eyes off Mal-lit-tay-lay. He was introduced to her plus a few other young squaws.

"Tom, you may court any of these as you please," the chief told him.

Next morning all the braves, with Tom and Pete, rode out to look for buffalo. They rode over one mountain, through pine timber and down into a valley. Two braves had ridden ahead to find a sign. They came back and reported seeing buffalo just over the next ridge. They cautiously crept over the hill where they could see the animals grazing. In one group they charged towards the buffalo, shooting as many as they were able to. Tom rode alongside a big bull and shot him with his rifle behind the front shoulder to bring him down. A brave went back to bring the women to help with the skinning. They moved the camp closer. Later that night they gathered around a fire beating a ceremonial drum dancing and singing. Tom couldn't keep his eyes from looking over at Mal-lit-tay-lay. *She's very pretty,* he thought.

Lo-oh-hee was giggling and whispering in Mal-lit-tay-lay's ear and pointing at Tom.

Pete noticed it and told Tom, "I'd wager you have a young maiden interested in you. Before long you should have a wife."

"Don't think so, Pete, not right now. Wouldn't want to take her on the run with me."

"You would be with the tribe and safe."

"Have to admit, Pete, that one standin' over by that young buck holdin' the Appaloosa is mighty pretty."

The girls were laughing and talking. They were looking over at Tom and Pete.

Lo-oh-hee whispered to Mal-lit-tay-lay, "I see the handsome half-breed keeps staring at you."

"If I get him for a husband, then you can have the older one in buckskins," Mal-lit-tay-lay laughed.

"No, I have eyes for Running Deer, and he is interested in me," Lo-oh-hee told her.

"We will give the one in buckskins to old Mal-tiene. She has no husband," Mal-lit-tay-lay giggled.

"Tom is coming this way," another girl announced.

Tom walked up to Mal-lit-tay-lay and said, “Let’s go for a walk and we can talk.”

“No, let us take our horses and ride away from camp,” she said.

Tom caught his horse and saddled him. She caught her own and swung up on him to ride bareback. She didn’t wait for him, but took off in a dead run, surprising him. He sunk spurs into his gelding and was fast closing the gap between them. When he came abreast of her she turned to look at him, throwing her long black hair over her shoulder and laughing, “I could have got away from you if I really wanted.”

They stopped at an opening that led into the forest. Tom dismounted, reached up and pulled her down from her horse. His muscular arms went around her waist, drawing her tight against him. Her body quivered as she felt the strength of his body against hers. She had felt so strong before and thought she was in control, but this man was making her feel like a woman. As his arms encircled her she felt weak and longed for his body. Tom laid her down in a grassy area and began kissing her. She was pressing her body against him with a strong desire. She wanted him and was willing for him to make love to her. He stopped and told her, “I want you for my squaw, Mal-lit-tay-lay. We’ll wait ’til your father gives you to me. I’ll have to give him gifts and right now I do not have anything. Where did you learn your English?”

“When I was very small I went to the mission school and stayed with some white people and they taught me. I want you for my husband, Tom. I will try to wait until my father gives me to you.”

He was fascinated with this wild and beautiful Nez Perce girl. They walked hand in hand to their horses. With no help from Tom she swung up on her horse and together they rode slowly back to camp. When Mal-lit-tay-lay dismounted, the other young maidens surrounded her.

“Did he kiss you and make love to you?” Lo-oh-hee asked.

“I will not tell you but I will say this. When he can give my father the right gifts I will become his squaw.”

“I envy you. If you change your mind and don’t want him, I will take him,” Lo-oh-hee told her.

"I will not change my mind. Tomorrow, Tom will talk with my father and ask for me, then he will tell him what he has to give," Mal-lit-tay-lay said.

Tom went back to where Pete and he were staying. The first thing Pete asked Tom was, "Are you goin' make Mal-lit-tay-lay your squaw?"

"I am, but I want to talk to her father in the morning an' I need you to translate."

"I'd be obliged to do that, Tom."

When the sun rose on the camp the next morning Tom and Pete walked over to Mal-lit-tay-lay's father's tepee. Her father, U-pok-pok (Gray Eagle), bending over, came out the low front opening with his daughter following.

"What does my Indian brother from the Shoshone tribe want with this old man?" He knew what Tom wanted but would wait for him to speak.

"I want your daughter Mal-lit-tay-lay for my squaw. What gifts do you demand for her?"

"Come back tomorrow and I will give you my answer," he replied.

Tom was hoping he would get his answer this day but he would have to wait.

"Until I give you my price, you may court her," he said.

Later on that day he went to her tepee and asked if she would like to go riding again. She was more than willing. In the warm afternoon they mounted their horses bareback and took off in the same direction they had gone yesterday. When they arrived at the same spot, Tom reached up, pulled her off her horse, and gathered her in his arms again. They sat down on a downed aspen and he pulled her close to him, kissing her passionately.

"I love you, Mal-lit-tay-lay."

She responded with, "I love you too, Tom. Let us make love."

"I want to, but we'll wait 'til your father tells me what his price is for you."

Tom wanted her but made up his mind he would wait.

She was disappointed, but she decided she would have this man whether her father gave her to him or not.

"Mal-lit-tay-lay, we better go back to camp. I will ask your father again if he has decided and what gifts he requires."

This time she let him help her on her horse. She wanted to feel those strong arms of his around her again. They took off in a gallop back to camp. They rode up next to her father's tepee. He was standing outside with Pete. He raised his arm in greeting and called him by his Indian name. Pete translated.

"White Eagle, I have decided. For six ponies you can have my daughter for your squaw."

"Pete, how am I goin' to get that many horses?"

"Probably have to steal 'em, Tom."

"Where would I do that, Pete?"

"Maybe we could steal 'em from some Blackfoot."

"I've never stole a horse in my life, Pete, except what we took from Judd an' his posse."

"From the Blackfoot it won't matter, Tom. I will talk to the chief about it."

"We have money, Pete. Do you reckon we could buy 'em instead?"

"No, I would guess the best would be to steal 'em. That's what we'll do. There're some Pend d'Oreilles around an' they're not at all friendly with the Blackfoot an' they more than likely will get the blame."

They walked over and talked to Alokut.

"The Blackfoot are not liked by us," he told them. "I will send two other braves with you to steal the horses, and they, like us, have fine ones. I have been told you have decided which maiden will become your squaw."

"Yes, Chief, he is like a young stud horse in love with a beautiful mare." Pete smiled as he said it.

"Mal-lit-tay-lay will make him a fine squaw and bear him many sons and daughters," Alokut commented.

Tom was anxious for the talk to end so he could go back and tell her what they were going to do to get the horses. Alokut could see he wanted to leave so he told him, "I see you are anxious to continue your courting. Why don't you go, White Eagle, and let Pete and me talk?"

Didn't take Tom long to hightail it back over to Mal-lit-tay-lay's tepee. She was sitting with some other maidens giggling and talking. She saw Tom and her eyes lighted up. "Do you want to go riding again?" she asked.

"Yes, let's go for a ride so I can tell you my plans."

They caught their horses, leading them instead of riding; they walked to the same place they had been yesterday.

"How are you going to get the horses my father demands for me?"

"Pete, two of the braves, and myself will go an' steal horses from the Blackfoot. We may have to travel a day to the north to find them. Don't know how long we'll be gone, Mal-lit-tay-lay."

"I wish you would not go. They are very dangerous Indians."

"We will watch when their young braves are away, capture the horses an' bring 'em back," Tom told her.

CHAPTER 15—POSSE AND INDIANS

The posse was traveling single file down a canyon, a steep rockslide to their left, aspens, poplars, and pines on the other side—a gentle slope to the top. A fast running stream ran down the center. The trail opened into a large grass filled meadow. Tracker Dan was riding ahead looking for sign. They had been following a trail chopped up from many horses. He sat his horse, took the makin's out of his shirt pocket, rolled a smoke, and was looking back down the trail waiting for them to arrive.

"Found where a tribe of Injuns made camp just last night. Don't know if they're with them but I'd be willing to wager they are. We're in need of the cavalry. Should have took the time, Judd, an' contacted the army, also the local law enforcement," commented Dan.

"I'm not wastin' time doin' that. We play our cards right, we'll get 'em. We stay out of sight an' watch. If we can get close enough for a rifle, I intend to kill 'em right where they stand," Judd told his deputies.

"I think it'd be better if we was to catch 'em away from the Injuns. If we shot 'em in camp, we'd have the whole tribe after us, an' I don't reckon that'd be smart. Don't care to have my scalp lifted," a deputy remarked.

"Let me tell you boys something. You're under my command an' you'll do as I say. None of you're gettin' out 'til we kill or capture those two. Don't reckon I've ever seen the likes of the men I have with me.

"Let's ride," Judd commanded.

They mounted up with the tracker in the lead and followed the tracks.

Two of the deputies riding at the rear discussed this chase. One of them turned to the other one and remarked, "The sheriff is crazy an' is goin' to get us killed an' scalped afore this is over."

"I'm in agreement with you but I don't how we're goin' to get out of this situation. We best watch an' be ready for whatever happens. Judd is too good with a gun to challenge him, an' I don't wager Dan will go agin him."

After leaving the meadows they entered white aspens with an occasional lodge pole pine mixed among them. Climbing a small knoll, they had a good view of the rolling hills ahead of them.

"I see smoke yonder maybe a mile. Could be an Injun camp," Dan told Judd.

"I aim to find a vantage point where we can see who might be in that camp," the sheriff said.

They rode the higher ground through the aspens and pines where they would blend in with the surrounding country. They climbed one hill to a ridge and found they could look down on whoever was down there.

"Sure could use a spy glass. I can see they're Indians but can't tell if Tom an' Pete are there. I'd be willin' to wager they are," Judd commented.

"Maybe I can get a little closer an' get a better look-see," the tracker remarked.

"You do that but don't let 'em see you," McCrea said.

Dan rode his horse a little closer, dismounted, tied him up and began to work his way closer, hopefully without being seen. He saw two riders riding toward him at a gallop. He lay down out of sight behind a downed aspen and waited. When they came close he couldn't believe his eyes; it was Tom and an Injun girl. Soon as they were out of range he crept back to his horse and rode back to the posse.

"Sheriff, I saw Tom with an Injun girl but couldn't see Pete. Didn't get any closer for fear of being spotted."

"We'll make camp far enough away so we won't be discovered, come back and watch the camp. Maybe we can catch one or both of them away from the Indians," Judd told them. "Mount up."

They moved back through the timber to a place where they might not be spotted and set up camp.

"Those Indians won't be movin' tonight, but one of us had best be up there an' keep a lookout on 'em," remarked the sheriff. "In the mornin', Dan, you go back where you was before an' watch the Indians' movements. Be no fire tonight. Too risky. Let's turn in. One of you deputies stand guard."

In the morning the tracker rode back where he could keep an eye out on the Indian camp. He found the spot where he had been before, hid and kept watch at the Indian camp in the distance. He hadn't been there long when two riders rode in his direction. As they rode closer, he recognized them.

Just as I suspected, it's Tom and that Injun girl again. Better get back and let Judd know. I know he'd have a clear shot here; don't think I like the idea of Tom getting killed. I have a feeling about Judd and this whole chase. I suspect there's more to it than just recapturing Tom and Pete. Judd has always seemed to have a lot of money, more than he could make on sheriff's wages, and he an' the judge seem to be mighty cozy. Besides as close to the Injun camp as we are, a shot would bring the whole tribe and I'd wager they'd lift every one of our scalps. I'll just tell Judd I haven't spotted 'em yet.

He crept back to his horse and rode back to camp. Judd spotted him and asked, "Did you see 'em, Dan?"

"No, Sheriff, they didn't leave the camp, leastways not in my direction. Saw three riding the other direction but couldn't make out who they were."

"We're goin' have to get closer to their camp where we can keep a better watch," Judd said. "There's a bluff over on the other side of their camp. That looks to be right where we can look down on the Indian camp."

"We best ride through the timber ahead of us so we'll be out of sight," Dan suggested.

They rode up a small hill covered with more aspens and pine, down the other side to a creek, following it until they were in sight of the bluff.

"We'll have to ride through a clear area before we're back in the timber again, and it's not very far to the Injun camp. We could be spotted an' we'd better hope none comes out this direction. We could be in for a fight if we're spotted. Don't dillydally around getting across," the tracker told them.

They made it into the timber again without being seen. It was steep and the horses were grunting, digging their hooves in, climbing up the side of the bluff. They were almost to the top when Judd slid over the rump of his horse, saddle and all. His cinch had broken and he went tumbling back down where they'd just ridden. After rolling a short ways, he got to his feet unhurt except for his pride. One of the deputies caught his horse.

"What's the matter, Sheriff, can't you stay on your horse?" Dan laughed.

"Shut up. I'm not in the mood for smart remarks from the likes of you." He retrieved his saddle and told a deputy, "Take this saddle on up to the top an' see if we can patch it up."

At the top they set up a temporary camp and Dan took a look at Judd's saddle.

"I reckon I can fix it, Sheriff. I'll cut some leather strings from the saddle an' that should make it good as new." *Too bad that didn't happen on that steep mountain we climbed yesterday. He might have rolled over the edge plumb to the bottom. He's gettin' to be a dangerous man an' afore this is through he's likely to get us all killed,* Dan thought.

"I'm goin' over on that large rock outcroppin' overlookin' the Indian camp. Might be able to look down into it," the sheriff told the deputies.

After he left one of the deputies remarked to the tracker, "Don't know about you, Dan, but we've got to do somethin' about Judd. He's gettin' mighty dangerous."

"I agree with you but right now I don't know what we can do. You know he's real fast with an iron. We'll just have to bide our time an' watch. Maybe catch him when he's asleep," Dan replied.

Judd found a place on a high rock where he could look down on the Indian camp.

Dan walked over and sat down next to him.

"Spotted anything, Sheriff?"

"Nothin' yet, but a lot of Indians goin' here an' there. Just a minute, I see two bucks on horses an' would you looky there. I see 'em. There's Tom an' Pete saddled up an' all four are ridin' out north. I wonder what they're up to. Let's get saddled up an' see if we can find their trail.

"You boys get those horses saddled. We're ridin' after Tom an' Pete," Judd told them.

With the sheriff and the tracker in the lead in the lead, they rode down the backside of the bluff. It was easy riding through the pine and aspens. At the bottom they turned north hoping to cross the riders' trail. They must have ridden three or four miles when Dan halted his horse and dismounted. He was kneeling down, looking at tracks. Turning and looking back up at the sheriff he said, " I reckon these are the tracks we're after. Two shod and two unshod horses. Don't know how far ahead of us they are."

Riding over a stretch of rocky hard ground, they lost the trail but later they encountered so many tracks they couldn't see which were from the four horsemen.

"McCrea, this ground is so chewed up with horse an' buffalo tracks, can't tell one from the other," the tracker told him.

"We'll ride in the direction we're on now," Judd instructed.

They rode over a timbered ridge and down below was an Indian camp. *Most likely a Blackfoot camp,* Dan thought. He turned in his saddle and said to Judd, "Don't see 'em an' I doubt if they'd ride into this camp since it ain't Nez Perce. I wonder where they're goin' an' what they're up to. Don't reckon it'd be wise to get any closer. Might have a fight on our hands. Must be a dozen tepees down there."

"Looks like they outsmarted us this time but not forever," remarked Judd.

"We best head back an' keep an' eye out on the Nez Perce camp. My guess they'll be back an', Judd, we're getting' mighty low on grub. We best see if we can get us a deer or elk. Better not be too close to the Injun camp shootin' anything," Dan commented.

"We'll keep a sharp eye out for some kind of game an' shoot it no matter where we're at," Judd ordered.

They were quite a distance from the Blackfoot camp when Dan spotted a young buck and shot him. "This'll tide us over for a spell I reckon," he said.

CHAPTER 16—NEZ PERCE AND THE BLACKFOOT CAMP

Standing Bear and Pa-kal-kay (Young Eagle) were leading them to the Blackfoot camp.. Standing Bear was medium height but stocky and muscular. He loved to wrestle. Young Eagle was six feet, lanky and a runner. He could stay on the trail of a wounded deer, running until he caught him.

They knew about where they would find the Blackfoot camp. After riding for a half-day, Pa-kal-kay motioned with his upraised hand to stop. "Pete, we're near the Blackfoot camp. We will have to get off, hide our horses, and sneak through the timber an' brush 'til we can see the camp. We must locate the horses and see if the braves are near."

With the two Nez Perce in the lead, Tom and Pete followed them as they rode silently through a stand of aspens and lodge pole pine towards the camp.

Standing Bear went ahead where he could see. He came back and told Pete, "The Blackfoot braves are away, most likely hunting buffalo. All I see are old men, women and young ones. On this side of camp in a grove of cottonwoods are the horses left in camp. There must be thirty ponies in a corral made of brush."

Young Eagle motioned for Tom and Pete to come forward. "We must be quiet when we go after the horses. Pete, you and Standing Bear will keep watch. Tom and I'll go down an' herd the horses in this direction. If they spot us, shoot into their camp. That should stop them until we're safely away."

Young Eagle and Tom rode as quietly as possible down the hill out of the pine and aspens toward the Blackfoot Indians' corral. A short distance from the enclosure, they dismounted and crept towards the horses. The Indians' horses smelled their horses and were nickering and milling around in the corral. If they kept it up they could be discovered, but they soon quieted down.

Young Eagle motioned to Tom. "Bring our horses and we will gather the Blackfoot ponies and be on our way."

He brought the horses and Young Eagle opened a pole gate. They rode in and hazed the horses towards Standing Bear and Pete. They started up the hill with about twenty horses, just what they could handle. Suddenly a shout came from the camp. They had been discovered.

"We've been seen!" Young Eagle shouted. "Move the horses fast and we'll out run them. It will only be young boys and old men after us. Maybe we'll shoot a couple and they'll be afraid to chase us."

They had the horses running, leaving the Blackfoot behind. They moved them over the timbered hill and down the other side to a meadow.

Mal-lit-tay-lay's father should find six good horses out of this bunch, Tom thought. *Shouldn't be long before she's my woman.*

The Blackfoot were nowhere in sight.

"If they come close to the Nez Perce camp they'll be afraid to come in. Maybe the Pend d'Oreilles will be blamed," remarked Standing Bear.

They ran the horses off and on until they reached camp. All the Nez Perce came out of their tepees to see the horses being brought in.

When the ponies settled down, Tom picked out six fine looking ones and led them over to U-pok-pok's tepee. The old man opened the flap and stepped out to see the horses Tom brought. "I see the young Shoshone has brought the horses to give me for my daughter. He has done well. I am pleased and accept the gifts. We must now prepare for the ceremony. There will be much dancing, singing and eating to celebrate.

Alokut was told the news. "He said this will be a fine day when we make the celebration."

They didn't know while stealing these horses, the sheriff and his men had been trying to catch them. Coming back with the horses they had been on a different trail.

The camp was preparing for the big feast when Mal-lit-tay-lay would become Tom's squaw.

"Tomorrow I will give my daughter to you, White Eagle," U-pok-pok told Tom. "Tonight we will dance and eat."

"Pete, where do you reckon Judd an' the posse are right now?" Tom asked.

"I have been wondering that same thing myself. He's not a man to give up. He wouldn't attempt to come into this camp. He's not a fool. Don't fret yourself about him, Tom. Tomorrow's your big day an' I envy you. I see Alokut coming this way."

"White Eagle, my Shoshone brother. Tomorrow you will be part of the Nez Perce tribe. Some of the braves are setting up a tepee away from the camp so tomorrow night you will be alone with your squaw. Young Eagle and Standing Bear are going to ride and find the buffalo for tomorrow's feast. Would you and Pete like to ride with them? You'll have plenty of time with your new squaw tomorrow."

"We'd be honored, Chief," Pete told him.

The two braves on their painted horses for this hunt joined Tom and Pete The four left camp riding east.

CHAPTER 17—ECOUNTER WITH THE POSSE

The posse had returned to the same place where they'd been watching the Nez Perce camp. Judd was sitting on a fallen pine looking down on the camp.

Dan walked up and asked, "Spotted anything, Judd?"

"Nary a thing yet, but I believe they're down there. I see some movement where their horses are. Look, there are four ridin' out. Looks like the same bunch as before. Maybe when they ride closer we can see who they might be. We're in luck. They're ridin' this way an' going to pass right under this bluff. I see who it is. Just the ones we want. Tom and Pete. Let's saddle up and get on their trail. Liked to shoot 'em right now, but that'd bring the whole tribe down on us," Judd said.

The posse headed down through the pine and aspens and cut across where they should find the tracks of the four. The tracker riding ahead stopped and waited for Judd and the posse.

Dan pointed down at some tracks. "It's them, Sheriff. No doubt of it. We best be careful now. There are four of 'em agin' us. Looks like they're ridin' towards those rollin' hills east of here, probably after buffalo."

The four horsemen's trail led the posse through some pine timber, aspens, and down a steep rocky mountain opening up into rolling grass hills. Beyond that were some low hills covered with more pine and aspens. Just out of the timber Judd spotted the four riders, maybe three hundred yards ahead. He motioned for the posse to stop. Quick as a cat the sheriff was off his horse, pulling his rifle out of the scabbard, and drawing a bead on one of the riders. He fired and one tumbled off his horse. He levered another shell and fired again. Another one slumped forward on his horse. The second one shot was still on his horse so he and the other two kicked their horses into a run and made it into the timber.

"I got two of 'em," Judd yelled with satisfaction. "Might have been Tom an' Pete. Let's go find out."

Pete felt the impact of the bullet as it knocked him off his horse. He knew he was hit bad when he looked down at his buckskin shirt and saw blood oozing down his chest. He had no idea where the shot came from or who had fired it. He heard the report of the rifle just as the bullet slammed into him. He reached down and pulled his pistol out of its holster. He would go down fighting. He heard riders approaching, and as one of them spoke, he recognized the voice. It was Judd McCrea.

The sheriff kicked the pistol out of Pete's hand and said, "Well just look what we've got here, and not in too good a shape. I told you, Pete, I would catch up with you," Judd remarked.

"You'll get yours eventually, Sheriff. You're nothing but a two bit thief and murderer," replied Pete.

"It won't be from you an' that's the sure-fired truth. You best be makin' peace with your maker because that wound you have will do you in, " Judd told him.

Dan stepped off his horse and was going to see what he could do for Pete. He didn't like this whole affair.

"Leave him be, Dan, he's done for an' I don't intend to make him comfy."

One of the other deputies remarked, "I don't like this. I never wanted a part of any killin'."

"Well you're in this whether you like it or not so just shut your mouth or I'll put a bullet in you and leave you here for the buzzards too," the sheriff told him. "Leave him be and let him die. We're goin' after the rest. I wounded one of them I'm sure. Let's get back on their trail."

They left him lying there and rode out with the sheriff in the lead. Pete was sure he was dying.

Tom and the two Indians made it into the timber. They found a place where they could make a defense and helped Tom down off his horse. The bullet had hit him high in the right shoulder.

Standing Bear told Tom, "We must get back to camp and treat the wound soon. We must be ready to fight whoever fired on us. I believe they'll be coming."

"It's probably the posse," Tom told them.

"We must get over behind those logs and defend ourselves," Young Eagle advised.

They picked Tom up, carried him over, and sat him behind a large fallen pine. He would be in a position of advantage and protection.

"I must stop the bleeding soon, Tom, or you'll bleed to death," Standing Bear said.

"When they come we'll fight. Give me my rifle," Tom told him.

"I hear horses," Standing Bear whispered.

"There, I see them down there in the aspens riding this way!" exclaimed Young Eagle.

"Prop me up so I can be ready to shoot," Tom asked.

They sat him on the ground behind the downed pine and gave him his rifle. They went off on each side to get the posse in a crossfire when they appeared.

When the first rider came around a pine, Tom fired and a deputy toppled off his horse.

"I got one of 'em. They're off their horses now and in the timber," remarked Tom.

"Better give up, Tom. I know you're shot bad," a voice hollered. Tom recognized Judd's voice.

"The odds have been evened up some, Sheriff, since I shot one of your men," Tom yelled back.

"Surrender, Tom, an' we'll let Pete go. He's bad off an' could use some doctorin'."

"I wouldn't believe you, Judd. Before this is through, I'm goin' see you dead an' the judge hung or put behind bars."

"For someone that's shot an' needs doctorin' his self, he's pretty sure of himself," Judd shouted.

"What makes you think I've been shot? When the Nez Perce come, you'll be outnumbered so I suggest you tuck your tail between your legs and head back to Silver City," Tom hollered back. "Another thing you can count on, Sheriff, you best keep an eye out on your back trail, 'cause I'm comin' after you to settle scores. I ain't dead yet by a long shot."

"Not goin' to happen, Tom. You're the same as dead right now. You won't get out of here alive, I promise you that. Enough of this jawin'. You've had your chance. We're goin' smoke you out," Judd yelled in response.

"I don't like this, Judd. You got one deputy gut shot. He won't make it through the day. You're soon gonna be all by yourself in this. I'm not about to rush 'em. There are only three of us now. You can charge 'em if you have a hankerin' to, but we're not," Dan told him.

"This one time I'd like some men with some backbone!" Judd fired back.

"Tom, you want to give up an' save a lot of bloodshed," the sheriff yelled.

Tom didn't answer him. He and the Indians were getting into a position to resist any rush by the posse. He motioned to Standing Bear and Young Eagle to move towards their horses and see if they could escape back to the camp.

"I think we have time before the posse decides to rush us, but if they do they'll meet with a lot of lead." The Indians understood by Tom's motions and the little bit of Nez Perce he had managed to learn what they would do. Standing Bear crawled over to Tom and helped him back into the timber where the horses were tied. Tom's shoulder was hurting but he knew they had to try to escape. *I wished I could do something for Pete but escaping and bringing the Nez Perce braves back is the only way.*

The two braves helped Tom on his horse and they quietly rode down the pine-covered hill to a creek. They traveled down the stream as far as they could before entering timber again. Tom's bleeding had slowed up some but they had to get back to their camp.

"I don't reckon the posse is close," remarked Tom.

"We will stay in the trees as much as we can on our way back to camp," Standing Bear told Young Eagle and Tom.

"We'll come back with some braves and see what can be done for Pete. It would be foolish for the white eyes to attack us," replied Young Eagle.

They were ten miles or so from their camp. They had to cross three open meadows and there was a danger, but they didn't have any choice.

"I believe the bleeding has slowed up," Tom told them.

"We're almost there; I see smoke from our lodges now," Standing Bear remarked.

As they rode through the tepees, the tribe came out to see the buffalo they brought, but were surprised to see that Tom was wounded and they brought no buffalo. Mal-lit-tay-lay came running and couldn't believe her eyes when she saw that Tom was wounded. Two braves helped him off his horse and into her tepee. Standing Bear went to get the medicine man. Tom was lying on a bearskin bed when the flap opened and Alokut stooped to enter with the medicine man following him.

"What has happened to my Shoshone brother?" he asked.

"Chief, we ran into the sheriff's posse. They shot Pete and wounded me. Don't know if Pete is alive or not. I must go back, find an' help him if he's still alive," Tom told him as best as he could.

"You will stay here and the medicine man will take care of your shoulder," Alokut said. "I will lead my braves and we will go back and try to rescue Pete."

CHAPTER 18—JUDD

Judd yelled out, "Tom, you might as well give up. We're comin' to get you. What's your answer?"

No response. "You know, Dan, I've a feelin' they've snuck out. You go on up there an' check it out. I'll keep you covered."

"Since it's your idea, Sheriff, you go get your head blown off. I'm not budgin'."

"All right, how about you, Deputy?"

"Not me either. I'm no fool. You want him so bad, why don't you go?"

"Since I've got lilly-livered men with me, I'll go an' you boys give me coverin' fire if I need it."

Judd moved out, skirting through some timber. No shots yet. Maybe he would take them by surprise. He walked beside a log and saw blood.

I would wager that's Tom's blood. Nobody around. He's got away temporally.

"You boys come on up here. They're gone. It's safe," he hollered.

When Dan and the deputy arrived, Dan remarked, "They'll be ridin' back to the Injun camp an' bring the whole tribe back. I think we ought to hightail it out of here whilst we have a chance, Sheriff."

"No, we'll ride back where Pete is an' if he's still alive, we'll load him on a horse an' take him with us for bargainin'. Might just trade him for Tom."

"I think me an' the deputy ought to leave you an' let you fight the Injuns all by yourself," remarked Dan.

"Any man that tries to leave I'll put a bullet in him," Judd told him.

"We've got to go back an' see what we can do for Deputy Baldwin," remarked Dan.

"All right, we'll see if Pete is alive an' try swapping him for Tom," Judd said.

They rode back where the deputy lay. Nothing they could do for him now. He was dead.

"We need to bury him, Judd. Since we don't have a shovel, we'll have to pile rocks on him to keep the wolves away," Dan said.

"You stay here an' cover him with rocks. Dan an' I'll go see if Pete is alive," Judd instructed him.

Judd and Dan rode back down through the timber to the edge of the meadow where Pete lay. He was still alive.

"Let's see what we can do for him, Dan."

Dan stepped off his horse and walked over where Pete lay still bleeding. Judd rode off to a place in the timber to find a place they could set up a lean-to.

"I'm going to try to help you. The sheriff wants you alive to trade for Tom," Dan told him.

"Pete, myself an' the one deputy left would like to get out of this an ' go home. The other one met the end on top the hill. Judd is goin' to get us all killed."

"I don't reckon I've much of a chance. Don't see there's much you can do for me. I'll tell you this, if the Nez Perce an' Tom make it back to the camp, you'll not have a chance," Pete said.

"I'm goin' to do what I can for you anyway," Dan commented.

"I'm obliged but I think you're wastin' your time," Pete told him.

Judd rode back over and told Dan, "We'll ride back up the hill an' send Deputy Brinks down to take care of Pete."

When they arrived at the top the deputy had finished piling rock on Baldwin's body.

"Go back down where Pete was shot an' see what you can do for him," the sheriff told him. "We're goin' after Tom."

With Dan in the lead they followed the tracks which led down the timbered hill where there was a creek.

Dan turned in his saddle and waved for Judd to come up beside him.

"They didn't cross this creek. My guess would be they rode down the creek for a distance and then came out somewhere downstream trying to throw us off."

"Maybe so. We'll ride down this stream an' find where they came out," Judd answered.

They had ridden a quarter of a mile when Dan pointed at the bank to his left. "There's tracks leading out an' I reckon it be Tom an' the Injuns. I would wager they are headed straight to the Nez Perce camp to bring braves back," Dan told him.

"That'll be fine since we'll do some parley'n with 'em on a trade for Tom," remarked the sheriff as they followed the tracks.

Dan turned and looked him right in the eye. "What makes you think they'll bargain with us? You're crazy, Judd. It will get us nothin' but killed an' you know it."

Judd had a wild mean look as he whipped his gun out, pointing it at Dan. "Hand over your pistol an' rifle. You're not runnin' out on me, if I have to kill you."

"When the Injuns attack you'll be fighting 'em all by your lonesome since I'm not armed. If I make it back to Silver City, I'll guarantee there'll be some changes. With your actions I'd wager you do have somethin' to do with the rustling an' maybe the judge also."

"Just shut up or maybe you won't leave here alive. As far as rustlin' there's no proof. When we reach the Indian camp, you'll go in an' try to make a trade. Don't try anything like joinin' the Indians because I'll be hidin' where I'll be able to see you an' I'll have a bead drawed on you."

CHAPTER 19—NEZ PERCE PARTY

The medicine man began working on Tom's wound. Mal-lit-tay-lay was by his side helping the medicine man. She refused to leave.

She leaned her head on his good shoulder and said, "I love you, White Eagle. You must not die."

"I will not die. I'm goin' after the sheriff an' I intend to kill him."

"No, the chief said you would stay here. He and some braves are going to see if they can get Pete back from the posse."

With Standing Bear and Young Eagle riding beside Alokut, they headed back to where the shooting took place. They and their horses were painted for war. A short time later Standing Bear spotted riders emerging from a timbered hill. Chief Alokut also saw them. He motioned for the braves to stop.

"It is the white men," he said. "We will wait and see what they want. Look, they must have seen us as I see a white flag. We will not kill them yet."

"I see Injuns, Judd, just like I told you. You're determined to get the rest of us killed," Dan told him.

"Don't fret yourself. This is better than I thought. Break out a white flag. This could be the chance I've wanted. Trade Pete for Tom."

Dan waved the only thing he had, a dirty kerchief, and the Indians stopped.

"You ride over to 'em and tell them we're willin' to do some tradin'. I will wait here whilst you palaver with 'em. If need be, I'll give you cover fire."

"That's real comforting. Why don't you talk to 'em, Sheriff?"

"Because you can speak some Indian."

"There are eight of 'em an' I don't reckon we'd have much of a chance agin' 'em," Dan remarked.

"They have stopped," Judd remarked. "Just get on with that flag of yours an' tell 'em our terms. Don't try any tricks 'cause like I said before, I'll have a bead on you 'an you'd be the first to die. Quit wastin' time an' move."

Judd handed him back his rifle. "Just in case you need it, Dan. Just don't try anything fancy."

Dan took the rifle and slipped it back into the scabbard, spurred his horse into a lope and with the kerchief raised, rode towards the Indians.

"Chief, I see one is riding this way with a white flag."

"Be watchful," Alokut told them. "I do not trust the white eyes."

Dan rode up to them and raised his hand in a greeting. Alokut raised his arm also and asked him, "What does the white man want? We know you have shot our brother Pete and also wounded our Shoshone brother."

"Chief, the sheriff wants to make a trade. He says he'll trade Pete for Tom. He wants to take him back to stand trial for murder an' escapin'. With care Pete may survive. The other deputy an' myself would like to give up this fight an' go back to our lodges an' family."

"You are outnumbered, white man, and your sheriff is a fool. We'll not give you Tom and we will take Pete back. I do not want wish to see more blood spilled so I tell you, release him, go back where you came from and we will spare your lives."

"I'll go back an' tell the sheriff what you said, but he's a stubborn man. I believe he'll kill us before he'll give up this fight."

Dan wheeled his horse around and in a slow lope rode back to where the sheriff was.

Pushing his hat back on his head and wiping his brow with the dirty kerchief, he told Judd what the chief had said. "I believe we'd best quit this fight an' head for home."

Pulling on his mustache, Judd remarked, "Maybe you're right at least for the time being. We'll ride back to Fort Missoula an' get the army involved. These Indians can't be allowed to break the white man's law. They should be taught a lesson. Ride back an' tell the chief, we'll leave an' he can have Pete. Tell him where he can find him."

With the kerchief waving in the wind, he rode back to where the chief and his braves were waiting. Riding up and gesturing with his hand he told the chief, "The sheriff will take your advice an' ride out, but I must warn you, he intends to ride to Fort Missoula an' bring the cavalry back."

"He is a fool," Alokut told Dan. "If he brings the soldiers he will die. You and the other man would be wise and go back to your lodges."

"We do not want to fight your tribe. The other deputy an' myself will leave the sheriff at the fort. You will find Pete close to where he was shot in a shelter we built. He was still alive, but he's in bad shape."

Dan reined his horse around and spurred his horse towards where Judd was waiting.

He pulled alongside the sheriff and said, "The chief said they'll let us go but warned if we brought the soldiers back there would be a fight."

"It might be a fight but the savages will lose. Let's ride back, get Brinks an' head for Fort Missoula," Judd told him.

The sheriff and Dan rode back up the timbered hill to the top and down the other side where Deputy Brinks and Pete were.

"Sure proud to see you boys. I was afraid the Indians might show up," Brinks remarked.

The sheriff and Dan dismounted and walked over to the lean-to where Pete lay. He could see he was still breathing.

"I believe I got his bleedin' stopped temporarily."

"Pete, we have palavered with the Nez Perce an' have decided not to trade you for Tom. I reckon you'll die afore long anyways. We'll ride to the fort an' bring the soldiers back so it's just a matter of time 'til I have Tom back or I have killed him."

Pete's breathing was labored and he was hurting. He didn't know if he was going to be able to hold onto life or not, but he responded to Judd. "I hope I'm alive when you come back because I want to see you dead."

"I don't reckon that'll happen with a passel of soldiers with us. We'll leave you now to your misery.

"Let's mount up, Deputies, and ride."

This time the sheriff took the lead. Dan and Floyd Brinks hung back at a distance talking. Dan was a thin, wiry man, six feet tall with a handlebar mustache. Brinks was a short heavy man built like a bull. Wouldn't back down in a brawl or a gunfight if he felt it was an honorable one, but neither felt this one was.

"What do you think of this whole situation?" he asked Dan in a voice low enough that the sheriff couldn't hear.

"I believe when we get to the fort we ought to desert McCrea. I have had my gut full of him of him leading us into sure death. He's crazy, Floyd, an' you know I'm inclined to believe he's involved in rustlin', an' maybe the judge also. He's obsessed with killin' Tom. He could be afraid he'd be found out, an' you know rustlin's a hangin' offence. Don't reckon normally he'd go to all this trouble tryin' to catch a man."

"I agree with you, Dan. If he can get the army involved, there'd be a battle an' maybe a start of hostilities with the Indians. Things have been on the uneasy side of late. It could happen."

The sheriff stopped his horse, turned and yelled back at them, "What'd boys hangin' back for? Wouldn't be wise if you're plannin' anything against me. Get on up an' take the lead, Dan, so's I can keep an' eye on you. I reckon you know the way to the fort."

Dan rode up alongside McCrea, stopped and looked him in the eye. "I think you're a fool to get the army into this. You could get all the Injuns on the warpath just because of your obsession catchin' one man. Why don't you just leave it be an' go back to Silver City?"

"I can surely see you'd never be a lawman. Most likely in a fight you'd tuck your tail between your legs an' run," Judd told him.

Dan's hand dropped to his gun but then raised it, deciding this was not the time to confront the sheriff. He knew Judd was fast and his better judgment told him not to try it now.

"Don't try it, Dan. I'd drop you afore your iron cleared leather." His eyes narrowed down to slits with a mean look in them.

"Some other time, Sheriff," replied Dan.

"Just do the job you were hired for, Dan, an' that's bein' a tracker an' deputy."

"We can't reach the fort before nightfall, Sheriff. I suggest we make camp an' get an early start come sunup. I see a place up yonder with water an' grass for the horses," Dan said.

"Very well, we'll make camp. Scare up some wood, Brinks, an', we'll have a little supper," replied Judd. "Remember, Dan, I'm a light sleeper so don't try anything."

Brinks had a fire going and coffee brewing. They all took jerky out of their saddlebags and poured themselves a cup of hot coffee. "Sure does hit the spot," Judd remarked.

Neither Brinks nor Dan said a word. Dan had come to hate this man, and Brinks now had the same feelings.

Before sunup they brewed coffee and ate jerky for breakfast.

"When we get to the fort, should get a decent meal," the sheriff said.

There was no answer to his comment from either Dan or Brinks. Dan was putting his saddle blanket on his horse, threw the saddle on his back and cinched it down tight. His horse swelled his belly up some. Didn't want the girth tight. Dan just waited 'til he relaxed and pulled up on the cinch strap, taking the slack out and climbed aboard. The other two were ready to ride.

"Take the lead, Dan, and, Floyd, you follow in behind him. I'd rather have you two in front of me. Should arrive at the fort this afternoon."

They had been riding for several hours up one timbered hill, down into grass filled meadows and several more just like the first when the fort came into sight. Upon arriving, Judd told a corporal at the gate, "I'm a sheriff from Silver City, Idaho, an' would like to see the officer in charge. Might you direct me to his headquarters?"

"Yes, sir, ride past the barracks on the right an' his office is just beyond; Captain Trace Parks be his name."

"Much obliged, Corporal."

They rode past the barracks and saw a building with a sign that said "Officer in Charge." The sheriff swung his six-foot-four frame off his horse, wrapped the reins around a hitching post, stepped up on the wooden porch, and knocked on the door.

An enlisted man answered his knock and asked, "What can I do for you?"

"I'm a sheriff from Idaho an' would like to see the officer in charge."

"Wait here an' I'll relay your request to the captain," he replied.

He came back a moment later and told the sheriff, "Come this way, the captain will see you."

The officer was a trimly built, smartly dressed man about five-foot-ten sporting a thin trimmed mustache that extended down the sides of his mouth. He was a West Pointer. When they entered the officer in charge asked him, "What can I do for you, Sheriff?"

"Captain, my deputies an' I have been on the trail of two men that are wanted for murder and escapin' from the law. They're presently with a band of Nez Perce an' they refuse to give 'em up."

"I don't know if I can help you. Just two weeks ago on June twenty-fifth, Sitting Bull and his Sioux wiped out Colonel George A Custer and his force of two hundred sixty-two men on the Little Big Horn. I'm expecting orders to proceed east and help quell the uprising."

"I was hopin', Captain, for a large force to put these Indians where they belong, either dead or on a reservation."

"Sorry I can't help you at this time with a large force. Even the Nez Perce are threatenin' to rise up against the white man. I can send one of my officers and two men to talk to the Nez Perce an' see if they can convince them to release the men to you."

"Very well, I'll accept your offer. How soon will your men be able to ride?"

"I'd say your group an' the cavalry should be ready to ride out in the mornin'."

"I'm obliged, Captain. Now we'd like a meal since our food has been scarce of late, an' supplies for tomorrow."

"In a couple of hours the enlisted men will be havin' mess an' you're welcome to join 'em. After breakfast the officer that'll be going with you will take you to the supply house."

He called his corporal in and told him, "Show the sheriff an' his men where the mess hall is located."

"Yes, sir," he said as he saluted the commanding officer.

"The corporal will take you to your quarters an' show you where you'll be havin' supper."

While the sheriff was talking to the commanding officer it gave Dan and Brinks a chance to talk privately.

"This is our chance, Floyd, to get away from McCrea an' go home afore he gets us killed. Right after breakfast we'll ride out. He won't dare try to stop us here."

"I'm be mighty obliged to get far from him," Brinks replied.

The sheriff walked out, following the corporal.

"You boys come with me. I'll direct you to the bunkhouse an' the mess hall."

They followed him to the bunkhouse and he introduced them to a couple of soldiers.

"We'll be havin' an officer and two men go with us to talk to the Nez Perce chief. He should be able to convince them to give up Tom so that the army don't come down on 'em," the sheriff told Dan and Brinks.

"I don't reckon they'll turn loose of him. You should have talked to the chief yourself, then you'd understand how determined the Injuns are," Dan replied.

"We'll get him back, I'll guarantee you that. Enough talk, let's go an' get some decent food."

They walked in with the soldiers through the line and were dished up food and poured a cup of coffee. They sat down with the other men at a table and the conversation they were heard was of the Sioux wiping out Custer's whole command. They may be ordered to ride east to quell the uprising. After eating they walked back to their quarters. Dan decided this was the time to tell Judd they were leaving for Silver City whether he liked it or not.

"Sheriff, tomorrow Brinks an' I are ridin' for home. You go an' get killed. We don't want anymore of your crazy idea of getting' Tom back. Those Nez Perce will wipe you an' your soldier boys out."

"You're in luck bein' on this cavalry post 'cause if you weren't you'd be dead. When I get back to Silver City, I'll take care of both you cowards."

"You may be fast with your iron, Sheriff, but I reckon I might be close to fast as you. I'll be ready for you if you're so lucky you don't get killed an' scalped by the Injuns," Dan told him.

Next morning after breakfast, Dan and Brinks gathered a few supplies at the army supply store and rode out towards the Lolo Trail and back home.

"If the sheriff manages to get out of this whole affair alive, you know he's goin' be gunnin' for us," remarked Brinks.

"I know but I believe with some practice I can outdraw him. The Injuns will probably do the job for me anyway."

Lieutenant Bufford sent his corporal to bring McCrea to him. When the sheriff was brought to him, he introduced himself. "I'm Lieutenant Nathaniel Bufford an' I will be in charge. I understand you have two deputies an' one that speaks some Nez Perce."

"I did, Lieutenant, but they both ran out on me. They have no stomach for a fight. Cowards I would say."

"I want to remind you, Sheriff, we're not goin' to fight the Indians. We'll try to negotiate for the release of the man you want. I do not speak any Indian but my corporal can, to some degree."

"Very well, maybe the presence of the army will convince him to hand over Tom and save bloodshed later."

"My men have been getting supplies for us an' I believe we should be ready to ride," the lieutenant told him. "Let's mount up an' ride over to supply."

They found the two enlisted men saddled with a packhorse ready to travel. They rode out following the officer and Judd, who were riding side by side.

They had not ridden far when a storm came upon them. Thunderheads had been building up over the mountains to the west. Just ahead of them lightning struck a tree and thunder rolled across the sky. Rain started coming down in torrents.

"We best find some shelter 'til this storm blows over, Sheriff," the lieutenant yelled over the noise of the storm.

"Surely you won't let a little rain stop you, Lieutenant? I want to get on to the Indian camp. They could have moved out of the country by now."

"I don't really believe so, Sheriff, but we'll move on 'til we get a little closer. With this weather we better make camp before too much longer."

"We can do that an' ride into the Indian camp early tomorrow mornin'. Hopefully you an' your soldier's presence will make 'em think twice before attackin' us."

CHAPTER 20—ALOKUT

Alokut and his braves followed the posse's tracks over the hill and down the other side where they found Pete. He knelt down beside Pete and said, "We are here, brother. We'll take you back to camp and tend to your wound."

Pete opened his eyes and muttered in a low voice, "I'm happy to see you, but I am dying."

"You will not die. Our medicine man will make you well. Standing Bear, make a travois for Pete to ride on."

They gently picked Pete up and placed him on the travois and rode slowly so as not to cause him any more pain than necessary, heading for camp. Reaching their encampment, they took him directly to the medicine man's tepee where Tom lay, then carried him inside.

Tom was improving and was sitting in an upright position when they entered with Pete.

"Pete, I'm happy to see you're alive."

He didn't hear him as he had passed out from loss of blood.

"Alokut, can the medicine man help him?"

"I do not know. He may need the white man's doctor to cut the bullet out, but we would have to get the army doctor at Fort Missoula. I do not trust the whites. Our medicine man will try to save him. He needs food so that he may get strength. Our women are making a buffalo stew that will make him strong."

The medicine man managed to stop the bleeding.

A low moan came out of Pete as he was beginning to stir. He opened his eyes and looked around and stopped when he saw Tom. "Is that you, Tom?"

"Yes, and I'm happy to see you're still alive. I was afraid you were dead."

"I thought the same about you, Tom, but I don't know about myself. The bleeding has stopped but I'm so weak I can't move."

"You don't give up. When the squaws get through pouring all that buffalo stew down your gullet, you'll be fit as a fiddle in no time."

"I want to regain my strength soon so I can ride an' kill that sheriff."

"You ain't goin' anywhere for awhile, but I'll be ready for the saddle before long an' I intend to kill him. Maybe I'll just bring his scalp back an' you can hang it from your lodge pole."

"Why don't you wait for me so that I could help you? You can't go up against a whole posse, an' the sheriff is a dangerous man."

"Don't you be concerned about me, Pete. I can take care of myself. I know Judd is fast with a gun but I'm goin' to practice 'til I'm as good or better than him. I intend to expose him an' the judge in the rustlin'."

"When Judd left me back there I heard him mention they were goin' to the fort to get the army involved," Pete said.

"Alokut knows that an' is prepared to fight. Don't fret about it. We may have to get the army doctor to take that bullet out. Someone will ride to the fort and bring him back, if he will come. Don't reckon you'd be able stand the ride there, Pete."

"If that be the case, you let a brave go fetch him. They'd most likely shoot you on sight an' you need to get well yourself," Pete said.

"No, I'm not in the shape to ride. I intend stayin' here 'til I mend."

"That is good, Tom."

The medicine man was trying to help Pete and even he knew the bullet had to come out. He told Alokut it would best if they brought the white man's medicine man to remove the bullet.

"I will send two braves to the fort an' see if he will come. They will be in danger because the sheriff has rode there for help. I hope there will be no trouble. I will send Standing Bear and Young Eagle," Alokut said.

He sent a young boy to fetch the two. When he came back with the two he told them, "I want you to ride to the fort and see if the white doctor will come back here to remove the bullet from Pete. You will go now but you must be watchful. You may see the soldiers riding this way. You will have to talk to them, as the doctor may be with them."

The young boy asked the chief, "Can I go with them?"

"No, you are not yet a warrior. You must wait," he told him.

The two braves rode out headed for the fort. The night before there was a big storm but today the weather had cleared. They had not gone far when Standing Bear spotted the soldiers riding their way.

"Look, I see three soldiers. I wonder what they want. They also have another white man with them. They have stopped and the man with them is getting off his horse. I can see he is a big man; must be the sheriff. They must have spotted us and he is getting his rifle."

"Let's get back in the timber quickly where we will have protection," Young Eagle said.

They galloped their horses back behind some large rocks.

Judd whispered to the lieutenant, "I see Indians." He dismounted, reached for his rifle and pulled it out of the scabbard.

"Hold on, Sheriff. Put that gun away. They don't look hostile to me. Maybe they're from the Nez Perce camp an' we can talk to 'em. Find out about the man you're after."

Judd slipped the rifle back and climbed back on his horse.

"We'll ride towards where we saw them. Carry a white flag an' see if they're still around," the lieutenant told one of the soldiers.

They moved in the direction where they had spotted the braves. The soldier was holding the white flag up hoping the Indians would see it and come out.

Young Eagle said, "I see the soldiers coming with a white flag. We must take a chance and see what they want. They may be able to tell us about the white doctor."

"Let us mount our ponies and go meet them and see what they want," Standing Bear said.

They rode out in the opening and waited as the soldiers approached them. When the soldiers rode up, the lieutenant raised his arm in greeting and Standing Bear acknowledged it by raising his arm also.

The officer turned to his corporal and said, "Ask him what tribe they belong to and if they're peaceful, as we mean them no harm."

The enlisted man turned to Standing Bear and asked, "Are you Nez Perce and is your lodge near?"

Standing Bear, puzzled, looked at Young Eagle and asked him, "Do you know what the soldier said?"

"No."

Young Eagle used some sign language. The corporal seemed to understand and with hand motions asked again the same question.

Young Eagle said to Standing Bear, "He wants to know where our lodges are and if he can talk with our chief."

"Tell him it is not far. We will take them. Then we can ask about the white doctor."

The corporal understood and turned to the lieutenant. "He said he will take us there."

"Very well, soldier; tell him we will follow them back to their lodges."

The Indians reined their ponies around. With the soldiers and the sheriff following they headed back to their camp.

"I don't trust these Indians one little bit. They may be leading us into a trap," Judd said.

"I don't believe so but we'll be ready just the same. We don't have any choice at this point," the lieutenant told him.

They rode over a timbered hill and down to a grassy meadow to the Indian camp. As they came down they were spotted, and everyone turned out to see the white men and the Nez Perce braves with them. They followed the braves through camp to Alokut's lodge. Stooping and throwing the flap back he emerged from his tepee.

The group stopped and the chief asked, "What are the white soldiers doing here, Standing Bear?"

"They wished to speak to you but I do not know what they want. Perhaps from them we can find out about the white doctor," Young Eagle replied.

"Tell the officer to come with me. We will go to Tom and have him ask them what they want."

The brave motioned for the lieutenant to follow the chief. Judd dismounted and started to follow also, but Young Eagle put his arm in front of him indicating he was to stay there. Alokut, with the officer following, walked towards Tom's tepee. When they reached it, the chief lifted the flap on the tepee and they entered. Nathaniel Bufford saw two wounded men lying there. One had dark skin and the other white. Alokut spoke to Tom and Pete. "This white soldier has something to say but we do not know what he wants. You must speak for us."

Tom spoke up. "What do you want? Are you here in peace?"

"Yes, if we weren't we would have the whole post here. I reckon you must be Tom. The sheriff wants to take you back to Silver City to stand trial for murder an' escapin' from the law."

"I am Tom, but he's lying! There's not a chance takin' me back. When I'm well the sheriff best keep an eye on his back trail 'cause I'll be comin' to kill him."

"If you won't give yourself up I may have to return with the whole regiment," he threatened.

"That would be a mistake, Lieutenant. Many soldiers would die," Pete spoke up.

"I will relay your message to the sheriff," the officer said.

"What did the white soldier want?" Alokut asked.

Pete repeated what he said and Alokut replied, "We will fight before we let them take you, Tom."

The lieutenant walked back to where the enlisted men and the sheriff waited.

"I'm sorry, Sheriff, but they refuse to give up Tom an' there's nothin' I can do. I think it best we return to the fort."

As they were standing there, Tom stepped out of his tepee. The sheriff saw him and his hand dropped to his pistol. He started to pull it out but the lieutenant saw what he was doing and grabbed his hand.

"Let go of my hand. I intend to kill him right now."

"Have you gone loco? You want to get us all killed? You leave that gun be or I'll have to put you under arrest," replied the officer.

"You go back to the fort 'cause I'm goin' lay in wait an' maybe I can catch Tom outside the camp."

"I can't let you do that since you're my responsibility. You'll ride back with us an' we'll report to the captain. Then it'd be my guess you'll be advised to forget this matter, as the army can't help you right now. I have told the chief there'd be no trouble from us an' he promised we'd be able to ride out of his camp an' no harm would come to us."

"All right, we'll go back to the fort an' I'll talk to the captain," replied Judd.

"I don't reckon that'll do you any good," Lieutenant Bufford told him.

The lieutenant walked back to the tepee where Pete and Tom were lying.

"When we get back to the fort, I will see if the captain will allow our doctor to come back an' take that bullet out," he told Pete.

"I would be obliged."

The lieutenant, the enlisted men, and the sheriff mounted up, heading back to the fort.

"It's late so we'll make camp before it gets dark. Private, you an' the corporal gather some wood for our fire."

They had traveled about halfway and the sun was starting to set. They found a place at the edge of some timber where they'd be reasonably safe should any Indians decide to attack.

"Sheriff, you will hand over your rifle an' pistol. In the mornin' I'll give them back to you."

The sheriff started to pull his pistol but immediately the enlisted men had their arms drawn and pointed at Judd.

"Don't believe it's a good idea. You'll not get your guns back now 'til we get back to the fort," the lieutenant told him.

"Corporal, you an' the private will take turns watchin' him tonight."

"Yes, sir," they replied.

Judd didn't try anything that night. The next morning they broke camp and rode towards the fort arriving in the afternoon. He was given back his guns and he and the lieutenant proceeded to the commanding officer's quarters. They were admitted to see the captain. The lieutenant snapped to attention and smartly saluted.

"What do you have to report, Lieutenant?"

"Sir, we talked to the Nez Perce and they refuse to give up Tom or the badly wounded Pete. There was nothing we could do but come back. Didn't want to start an uprisin'. They requested the services of our doctor to remove a bullet from Pete."

"You did right, Bufford. I look to receive orders to ride for the Little Big Horn at any moment. Sheriff, you'll have to give up this chase an' go back home. We can't help you at this time. I personally have my doubts of the guilt of this man."

"I'll ride back to Mount Idaho an' see if I can round up a posse," the sheriff said.

"If you do that, you'll start an Nez Perce uprising for sure an' get a lot of innocent people killed. If I catch you back in Montana I'll arrest you an' put you in the stockade. I want you on your way to Idaho at the crack of dawn."

"I can see you don't have much law here in Montana." McCrea was a stubborn man but he could see there wasn't anything he could do. *I'll go back to Silver City and take care of Dan an' Brinks. I have a gut feelin' that all I have to do is wait an' Tom will be comin' back,* he thought as he turned and walked away from the captain.

Early next morning, with a small pack of grub on his horse, the sheriff stepped into the saddle and rode out towards the Lolo Trail. He was now by himself.

The corporal and the medical officer left for the Nez Perce camp. Riding hard they reached the Indian camp after dark. They rode right in with no trouble as the soldier was recognized. They were taken to Alokut's lodge. Following him, they walked to Tom and Pete's tepee. Alokut lifted the entrance flap and with the doctor behind him, entered leaving the corporal standing outside.

"I'm glad to see you, Doctor. I know this bullet has to come out or I will die for sure," Pete said.

"Yes and I can see the wound's infected. I will remove it but there's a chance you may die anyway. Tell the chief to bring the soldier. I'll be needing his help an' we'll need hot water. I brought a bottle of whiskey to disinfect the wound also."

"Before you start, Doctor, how about a big shot?"

"I reckon we can do that. Hand me the bottle, Corporal." He gave it to Pete and he took a long, hard drink before handing it back.

"You will be out, Pete, and will not feel a thing." He put a cloth soaked in chloroform over Pete's nose and mouth, and moments later he was asleep. The doctor began probing for the bullet and before long had it in his forceps. He poured whiskey on the wound after closing the incision.

"We'll wait for him to awake. Don't know if he'll live or not. Matter of just waiting."

He asked Tom to tell the chief there was nothing more he could do now. "Make sure his wound is kept clean an' get plenty of that buffalo stew into him. It will give him strength. We can't do anymore here an' we need to get back to the fort. Let me take a look at your wound."

He examined Tom's shoulder and told him, "The medicine man did a fine job. I reckon you're going be just fine. The bullet passed right on through the shoulder. Just keep it clean is my advice."

"I'm obliged for what you have done, Doctor."

"Just doing my job, son."

Alokut through Tom, thanked the white doctor for what he had done and told him he would have an escort of braves for part of his return trip. As they left the tepee the Indians had their horses ready for them. They rode out with six braves accompanying them.

CHAPTER 21—BLACKFOOT

The Indian women had been feeding Pete a lot of Buffalo stew and he was gaining strength. It was almost the end of August. A regiment from Fort Missoula had left to help quell the Sioux uprising.

"Pete, we hear the fort is almost empty of troops an' it's been 'bout two weeks since the army doctor removed that bullet. You're lookin' a sight better now. I'm goin' to be leavin' for Silver City before long to settle scores with that sheriff," Tom remarked.

"You just hold on 'cause I'm goin' with you. I have a settlement to make with Judd myself."

"Don't think so, leastways not at this time. The Nez Perce are goin' be headed back to the Wallowas most likely in September."

"You can't be a goin' against McCrea by yourself. You know he's fast an' cunning like a rattlesnake. His aim is to kill you an' he more'n likely would have help. You bide your time an' I'll be fit to go with you. We could get the Bar-0-1 hands to help clean up the town. They were goin' to rustle back the cattle. I wonder if they managed to do that."

At that moment Standing Bear burst into the tepee. "We are being attacked!"

"Soldiers?" Tom asked.

"No, Blackfoot."

He left in a hurry with Tom following. All of the young Nez Perce braves had gone to hunt buffalo. Only old men protected the camp. Emerging from the tepee, they could see Blackfoot galloping through the camp, shooting arrows at everyone they saw. The smell of gunfire was heavy in the air. Two braves saw Tom. They were whooping and shouting as they rode in a gallop towards him. Tom shot one and he fell from his horse. The other jumped off his horse and was on Tom, swinging his war club at him. Tom was knocked down but pulled his knife and sunk it into the Indian's chest. He ran to Mal-lit-tay-lay's tepee. There was nothing but pandemonium. Lo-oh-hee was screaming, "They have taken Mal-lit-tay-lay and two other girls."

"What direction did they ride?"

She pointed towards the north. "That way. Hurry! Catch them and bring them back. Kill the Blackfoot."

To the east, the Nez Perce braves were returning from the hunt. They heard the shooting. Riding as hard as their horses would go, with Alokut leading, they entered camp in time to join in the fighting. They killed several of the enemy and the rest escaped with the Nez Perce in pursuit.

Alokut swung down from his black spotted Appaloosa, saw Tom and asked, "What girls did they take?"

"Mal-lit-tay-lay and two others. I'm leavin' now."

"No, you will stay here. Our warriors will go after them."

"I'm going with you."

"Very well, we will ride," he said, as he swung up on his horse.

Alokut, with Tom and twenty braves, rode out on the trail of the abductors. The Blackfoot trail was easy to follow.

"We should be close to the Blackfoot camp. They will be expecting us to be coming in from the south. A few of our braves will ride in from that direction. The rest of us will fool them and come in from the north. We will show no mercy," Alokut told them. "Tom, you will stay back in the rear."

"I cannot do that, Chief."

"Your foolishness will get you killed."

One of the braves scouting ahead rode back and reported, "The Blackfoot camp is just over that hill you see in the distance, and it appears they are prepared to do battle with us."

"We will wait on the hill north of their lodges and as soon as our braves attack from the south, it will be time for us to attack."

They did not have to wait long. From their vantage point on the hill looking down, they saw the Nez Perce warriors attacking and the Blackfoot meeting their adversaries in battle.

"Let us ride now and send the Blackfoot to the happy hunting grounds." Alokut yelled a war hoop as he galloped down the hill with his braves and Tom following.

They entered the camp whooping, hollering, and shooting arrows and guns at every Blackfoot man they saw. Women were screaming and the braves were yelling. Tom jumped off his horse and started searching every tepee. A warrior came at him with a war lance but Tom shot him, and he fell before reaching him.

"Where are you, Mal-lit-tay-lay?" Tom yelled but there was no answer.

He went from tepee to tepee while the others were engaged in battle. He entered one and looked over and there she was with two other Nez Perce girls, bound and gagged. He started for her but someone hit him from behind and everything went black. Alokut burst through the opening just as a Blackfoot warrior was about to open up Tom's head with a tomahawk. He sunk his knife into his back. Alokut knelt down and rolled Tom over on his back, checking to see if he was alive. Tom groaned as he came to, striking out, but the chief grabbed his hand.

"Tom, my foolish Shoshone brother, you almost got yourself killed going off by yourself."

"Where is Mal-lit-tay-lay?" Tom asked.

"She and the other maidens are alright. They are sitting over there on the other side of the fire still bound and tied. Your squaw is waiting to be untied. You better go untie her. I can see in her eyes she is getting very angry."

Tom crawled over to her, untying the other two first. As badly as his head hurt, he wanted to enjoy this moment so he took his time. Finally undoing her bonds she said, "You can make this Indian girl so mad," but her rage quickly left as she threw her arms around him. "Don't you ever leave me again," she said.

"Come, let us go back to our camp. What Blackfoot we have not killed, the rest have run away," Alokut told them.

As they emerged from the tepee with the captive girls, Standing Bear rode up. "Have we lost any braves?" the chief asked him.

"We have not lost any, but two braves are wounded. It has been a good day for battle," he remarked.

"We will ride back to our camp and prepare for Mal-lit-tay-lay to become Tom's squaw," Alokut told them.

Tom's shoulder had healed and preparations were being made for the wedding. Tonight would be the ceremony with feasting and dancing. Guards were posted around the camp to watch should the Blackfoot return. Tom walked over to Mal-lit-tay-lay's tepee and told her, "Let's go for a walk."

She took hold of his hand and they walked down to the little creek that flowed by their camp. They sat down on the grassy bank and she said, "Tomorrow we will stay in our tepee at the edge of camp where no one will disturb us for five days. We will make love and I will cook for us."

That night the dancing began with the dancers in their colorful outfits dancing to the drummer's beat and singing songs of joy. The scent of buffalo being roasted over the open fire was wafting through the air. The cooking of chokecherries and many other good smells drifted through the camp. Tom danced and the women did also. Late that night after much food, Alokut called Tom and Mal-lit-tay-lay to stand before him. He recited chosen Nez Perce sayings and announced to him, "She is now your squaw, Tom. Take her to the tepee that has been prepared for you at the edge of camp."

She was grinning as she took him by the hand. "We will now go to our tepee and you will make love to me." She threw the entrance flap back. Tom followed. Once inside she turned and threw her arms around him. Gently laying her on a bearskin rug, he began kissing her passionately. He slowly began to remove her doeskin dress. He ran his hands over her smooth brown naked body, noticing how beautiful she was. Then the night of lovemaking began. It went on until the early hours until they both fell asleep. When he awoke she fixed him something to eat, but before he could get up, she slipped off her buckskin dress and crawled into their bed. Putting her arms around him, she said, "You can eat later. Let us make love again." Afterwards he fell asleep and when he awoke she was fixing him some food. He awoke and dressed. She came to him and he put his arms around her.

"I love you, Mal-lit-tay-lay."

"I, too, love you," she said.

They made love for five days, but the time had come when the tribe would be going back to the Wallowas. Alokut came to their tepee and told them, "Tomorrow we will ride back to our home. Will you stay with us, Tom?"

"I will until we reach the Snake River. I'll have Mal-lit-tay-lay go with her family an' I'll ride to Silver City for my revenge. Then I'll return to your people who are now my people."

"You are a very foolish young man. If my brother, Chief Joseph, were here, he would advise you as I do. We cannot help you in your revenge. Our relations with the white man are not good and there is talk of war if the white man tries to move us out of the Wallowas to a reservation. What will you tell your squaw?"

"Nothing 'til we reach the Snake."

The next morning all the lodges were torn down and preparations made for the long trip home. It would be ten days to two weeks before they reached the Wallowas. Pete would be carried on a travois, as he was not yet strong enough to ride.

CHAPTER 22—McCREA AND THE JUDGE

The sheriff stopped in Mt. Idaho, rode over to a man on the street and asked where he might find the local law.

"Just down the road a short piece on the right, you'll see the brick building. That's where the jail is, an' his office."

"Much obliged," he said as he touched the brim of his hat.

He reined up in front of the jail, swung his tall body out of the saddle and walked in. The local sheriff looked up to see who it was.

"What can I do for you? I see you're wearin' a badge. Might you be that lawman that came through sometime back asking questions? Seems to me you had several men with you an' were on the trail of two men. If I recollect, you caught them but they overpowered you an' your posse at the Clearwater an' you walked back to Mt. Idaho," he said with a grin.

"That's correct, Sheriff. They did get the drop on us. I'm a lawman from Silver City an' I need a posse to ride with me to Montana. One of my men was killed an' four others didn't have the backbone an' skeedaddled for home. Cowards. That just leaves me."

"How come you didn't scare up some men in Montana?"

"I tried to get the army involved but most left for eastern Montana to fight Indians."

"Mighty strange, Sheriff. I'm right sorry but can't let you have any men here, as most are on the alert because of the Indian unrest. Don't reckon any of the locals would go with you."

"As I see it, I'll have to go south to Silver City an' maybe find some men willing to go after these murderers," Judd said.

"Sorry I can't help you at this time. I can't leave to hunt anyone down the way things are now."

Judd turned around and not saying a word walked out the door, swung into the saddle and headed out of town. *What's the matter with the men around here? Appears to me they're all yellow.* He rode by the local bar and decided to have a drink and something to eat. Dismounting, he tied his horse to the hitching rail, stepped up on the boardwalk and pushed the batwing doors open. The smell of cooking steaks was in the air. He walked to the bar with the big Mexican rowels on his spurs jingling.

The barkeep asked, "What'll it be, whiskey or beer?"

"Give me a whiskey and a big steak."

After eating he walked out, put his foot in the stirrup and swung aboard his horse, heading south.

Judd had been riding for two days. He didn't stop at Council figuring he would stop at Rafe Anderson's ranch in Indian Valley for the night. Riding down the long grass and sagebrush- filled mesa hill, he spotted the ranch at the north end of the valley. It had rained the night before and the pungent smell of sage was in the air. He rode up to the front gate, dismounted, walked to the front door and knocked. Mrs. Anderson came to the door.

"Well, hello, Sheriff. It's been quite a spell since we last saw you. Did you get the men you were chasin'?"

"No, ma'am, but I surely will in time."

"Would you care to join us for supper an' stay the night? I reckon you must be headed back to Silver City?"

"That I am. I would be obliged, ma'am, to take supper with you folks. I'm a sight sore from all the hard ridin' I've been doin' since leaving Montana."

Mr. Anderson came in from working the fields and greeted the sheriff. "You look all tuckered out. Sit down there on the porch swing an' rest yourself 'til supper's on."

"That's be mighty pleasin' to my body right now. I'm plumb wore out from chasin' those men all over the country."

Mr. Anderson pulled out his pipe, stuffed it with tobacco, struck a match lighting it, and asked, "What happened, Sheriff? Did you finish takin' care of those two you were after?"

"I shot both of them but they took shelter with a band of renegade Indians an' the army refused to go in after them. I have a gut feelin' one or both will be comin' back to Silver City afore long, an' when they do I'll take care of them once an' for all."

Mrs. Anderson stepped out on the porch and announced, "Supper's on the table, boys."

"We eat breakfast early, Sheriff, an' I expect you'll want to be on your way."

"Yes, ma'am, I reckon it'll take me most of three, four days to reach home."

Right after eating at daybreak, Judd saddled his horse, climbed aboard and with a nod rode south. Two days later he encountered two Indians along a river trail. They gave him a peace sign, but he told them, "I don't like Indians, an' you're in my way." He shot them both, not giving them a chance. On the fourth day he rode into Silver City and went right to the judge's house. Dismounting, he walked up to the steps and knocked. Judge Potter came to the door and remarked, "Where have you been all this time? Did you get Pete and Tom?"

"No, but I shot them both"

"That's good. We won't be bothered with them. Four of your deputies came back. Dan an' Brinks were the last two. They said you had gone plumb loco. They reported to me one of your deputies was killed in Montana. Sorry to hear that but that's the danger of being a lawman. Now that you're back you can take care of those Bar-0-1 hands. Some of our cattle have been rustled an' I suspect it was them."

"Tom is not dead. Pete may be though. They took refuge with some Nez Perce an' the army refused to help me arrest them."

"You are an' imbecile, Sheriff. What if he comes back here?"

"That's what I'm countin' on. Then I'll take care of him once an' for all. I've got some other business to take care of after I rest up some. Then I just reckon I'll go find Dan an' Brinks. I have some unfinished business with them. I'll talk to you tomorrow, Judge."

"Don't believe you'll find Brinks. I heard he left town."

"Dan is the one I want. Got a score to settle with that yellow belly."

"You might check the hotel bar. Heard he's been there a lot these days getting' drunk, an' folks have said he's been practicing drawin' his pistol."

"I'll just do that after I rest some. If he's intendin' on comin' against me, I'd say he's downright foolish."

In the morning he walked over to the hotel and ordered breakfast. He was eating when Dan came in, saw McCrea and strode towards him.

"I'm surprised you didn't run out of town, Dan. You know you can't outdraw me. Right now I'd like to finish my breakfast an' if you've of a mind to, I'd suggest you leave town while I'm in a halfway good mood. Besides, it would be good for your health."

"I told you, McCrea, in Montana the day would come when I'd even scores with you an' that's what I'm aimin' to do right now."

"You're a fool. You know you ain't no match for me, even if you have been practicin'."

"You just get outta that chair an' we'll sure as hell find out."

Judd pushed his chair back and stood up. People moved away from their tables, giving them room.

"I've been hopin' you would get back so I can settle things with you," Dan said.

"I'm surprised you didn't skedaddle out of town like a rabbit just as Brinks did."

"He may be afraid of you but I'm not," replied Dan.

"You'd best be 'cause this is the day of reckonin'."

"This is one time you ain't goin' bully me."

Dan's hand dropped to his gun and as it cleared leather, the blast from Judd's gun erupted and the bullet hit Dan just below the rib cage. He dropped to his knees and with a puzzled look, he uttered as he fell forward, "I didn't think you could outdraw me."

Judd sais, “Some of you men over there, drag this man outta here.”

He walked out and went to his office. He was sitting there going through some papers when Judge Potter walked in. “I heard what happened at the hotel. That’s not goin’ to set too favorably with the townsfolk.”

“Judge, it’s an open an’ shut case. He drew on me. If you do your part, there won’t be any trouble.”

“Very well, I’ll take care of it. In the meantime you better a ride out to the box canyon where we’re holdin’ the cattle an’ see that they’re taken to market.”

“Have someone keep an eye out for Tom. I’d bet a double-eagle he’ll come back. Inform me soon as he shows up. I’m goin’ get rid of him once an’ for all.”

“You stay away from the Bar-0-1 Ranch. They might like to catch you in Oregon,” the judge told him.

CHAPTER 23—TOM AND SILVER CITY

Tom and the Nez Perce had reached the Snake and were preparing to cross. Tom came to Mal-lit-tay-lay, took her by the hand and led her off away from the others.

"You are going to stay with your people for awhile an' I'm ridin' back to Silver City to settle scores with the sheriff."

"No, Tom, do not do this. I will not let you. You will surely be killed. Stay with my people and you will be safe."

"I'll never be safe as long as he's alive, so I must go."

"You are so foolish. I will never see you again."

"This should not take long an' I'll be back."

This time of the year the river was low. The Nez Perce began their crossing. Wouldn't be long before they'd be back in the Wallowas. Mal-lit-tay-lay was crying as she watched Tom ride off. She just knew he would be gone forever. He felt emptiness as he rode off, but he knew he had to avenge himself because Judd would always be after him. He was riding the same trail that the sheriff had ridden not long before. He rode into the Anderson ranch in the evening just as the sun was setting behind the mountains in the west.

He rode up to the house, dismounted and tied his horse to a hitching post in front. Mr. Anderson came to the door.

"Light down off that horse an' come in. The sheriff has been through here an' he told us what happened in Montana. He's none too happy. He figures you'll be returnin' to Silver City an' he says he's goin' to kill you. Are you ridin' to Silver City?"

"Yes, to even scores with the sheriff."

"I think you're makin' a mistake an' may get yourself killed, but I reckon you're set in your mind about it. We're about ready to sit down for supper an' you're welcome to join us. I reckon you'll want to spend the night."

"I would be pleased for a place to lay my head."

Mrs. Anderson said, "We have an extra bed for you upstairs. You can stable your horse in the barn."

"I'd be much obliged, ma'am."

The night air was getting cool as darkness came. They couldn't believe this man to be dangerous, as the sheriff had told them.

"I reckon I'll go to bed as I still have a long ride ahead of me."

Tom walked up the stairs to his room, unbuckled his gun belt and sat down on the bed. It had been a long time since he had felt anything so soft.

He arose early and walked down the stairs to the kitchen where Mrs. Anderson had breakfast set. He could smell the hotcakes and bacon being cooked. He was certainly hungry.

"Sit down, Tom, an' dig into those pancakes."

After breakfast Rafe headed for the fields. Tom saddled his horse, thanking the Andersons for their hospitality, stepped up into the stirrup, threw his leg over and was in the saddle. He spurred his horse into a slow lope was on his way again for Silver City.

Crossing the Snake River far south of where the Nez Perce had crossed, the land became broken hills, sagebrush and canyons. As his journey took him south, the juniper trees became more numerous and in the mountains there was a scattering of small pine. He rode down a canyon with sheer rock walls on each side, with a few pine trees hanging on to what little bit of soil they could find. He was following an Indian trail that was also used by whites. There was a small, fast-running creek with green grass and poplar trees where he would make camp. A gentle breeze was blowing through the canyon. This would be the same route that the sheriff would have taken, and not long before.

The next morning he rode into Henry Fetterman's horse ranch. As he rode through the front gate he was met with a man with a rifle.

"It's me, Henry, Tom Sikeston."

"Well I'll be doggoned. What are you doin' back in this part of the country? You know Sheriff McCrea is expectin' you to come back."

"That's what I've been countin' on 'cause I'm lookin' for him an' I intend to kill him. He's put one bullet in me."

"The talk is, Tom, he's plannin' on you showin' up an' he's set on killin' you. No puttin' you in prison. He's mean an' dangerous. The whole town needs cleanin' up but it'll take more than one. The whole town is under his thumb. Everyone's afraid of him. I think he's gone crazy since he killed Dan Wilkerson, an' Dan was fairly fast too."

"I reckon I've got a fair chance. I've been practicin' an' I think I'm a match for him. He draws fast but hesitates a mite before he pulls the trigger. That's what I've been told, an' I believe that'll be my advantage. I may not be as fast on the draw but it's important that I be accurate. That one second could run to my favor. He'll also be expectin' me to ride into town from this direction, but instead I'll take the old juniper trail an' come in from the south."

"I know you've got your mind set on this but I'd rather see you standin' and not in a pine box. You be mighty careful, son."

"I'll just do that, Henry. I best be on my way."

Judd was headed for the hotel to get a drink and something to eat when he saw Judge Potter waddling his short, fat body toward him, waving. Judd despised this pompous little fat man but would put up with him for the time being.

When Potter reached the sheriff he was out of breath but managed to blurt out, "Tom's been seen in town, Sheriff."

"Where was he seen?"

"Down at the south end of town about thirty minutes ago."

"Did anyone talk to him?"

"Not that I know of. He went into the gunsmith's from what I understand."

"I'm goin' to go ahead and have some grub an' a drink. I reckon he'll find me when he's ready, an' I'll be waitin'."

"You make sure you kill him, Judd, before he goes to get the Bar-0-1 hands. Don't want him bringing them in."

"Don't you worry your fat little body none. You just go take care of your business an' I'll worry 'bout mine."

Potter didn't like the remark, but what could he do about it? *After this is over I need to find someone to take care of the sheriff. He has gone crazy.*

Tom entered the gunsmith shop. The owner was bent over his worktable working on a rifle. He looked up when Tom walked in.

"Can I help you, young man?"

"I'm in need of some ammo for this .45 peacemaker an' maybe a .44 repeating rifle, depending on the price."

He turned around and took a Winchester off a rack. "Here's a nice rifle. It has good action an' would get the job done. You're Tom, the fella the sheriff is after, ain't you?"

"That's right. Do you have any problem with that?"

"No, sir. You must be here to shoot it out with the sheriff? You'd be doin' us a favor gettin' rid of him. He says he's made this town safe for the citizens. He sure has all right. He runs the town the way he sees fit. A person doesn't dare cross him or he's dead. Tell you what, young man. Why don't you take this sawed-off double barrel 12-gauge? I'll even let you have it on credit. It'll bring him down to size."

"I'd be obliged. I'm here to even up scores. He put one bullet in me an' nearly killed my friend. I'm leavin' now. You keep shut about me bein' here. I more 'an likely have been spotted already."

"You don't have to worry none about me. Go out the backdoor. Less chance bein' seen."

Tom did just that and started walking towards the hotel. He met a man coming towards him.

"Have you seen the sheriff?"

"I saw him at the hotel awhile back but he left and headed over to the jail. He mentioned that you were in town lookin' for him. I reckon he's plannin' on killin' you, Tom. Don't believe he's got anyone on his side though. The folks around here have pretty much soured on him, exceptin' the judge. Even Vernal an' Will have backed away from him."

"I'll find him."

Tom started walking towards the jail, up the dusty street, and past a livery stable on his right and a millinery store across the street. When he arrived in front of the jail he yelled, "Come on out, Judd."

There was no answer. Might be an ambush he considered. *I best get out of the middle of the street.* Before he moved a voice came from within the jail. "Don't shoot. I'm comin' out."

It wasn't Judd's voice.

"Whoever it is, don't try anything," Tom hollered.

The outer door of the jail opened slowly and a young man came out.

"I'm just tendin' the jail for the sheriff. He ain't here."

"Where is he?"

"He said to tell you he'd be down at the funeral parlor. Wanted you close so there wouldn't be too much trouble puttin' you in a pine box."

Tom turned around without saying another word and headed for the parlor. He walked a couple of blocks and made a turn on a street to his right. There were several buildings between him and where the sheriff was supposed to be. He made it just past the second building when a shot rang out and a bullet imbedded itself in the wood of the door right beside him. He jumped into a space between two buildings. The shot came from high. He peered around the corner, looking up on a roof when a head and rifle appeared and pointed down at him.

Tom fired and the man tumbled off the roof. It was not Judd.

He yelled, "What's the matter, Sheriff? You need help?"

There wasn't any answer. *Maybe he's playing it safe and has some help.*

He went on between the buildings, planning on coming around behind the funeral parlor. Just as he came around the building another shot rang out and nicked Tom in the arm. He hollered and a man stepped out of the shadows, thinking he had taken care of Tom. Tom moaned and the man started across an opening towards him.

"You still alive? You won't be long." The man had his rifle in his hand.

Tom stepped around the side of the building, surprising him. The cowboy who nicked Tom raised his rifle to shoot just as Tom fired his pistol from the hip, hitting the man in the belly. He went down. He screamed in pain, "I'm hit!"

Tom walked over to him and asked, "Where's Judd?"

"He's in the parlor. I need a doctor bad. I'm going to bleed to death."

"Go ahead an' bleed, but right now I want to know if there are more than two of you helping the sheriff."

Through his groaning he answered, "There was three of us with Judd."

"I shot the one on the roof. Now where's the third man?"

"It's not a man but a woman, and she's right good with a rifle or pistol."

"Where's she at? I never shot a woman before but this just might be my first time."

"She's hidin' in the front room in a pine box an' Judd is in the backroom. She figures on getting' you from behind as you walk to the backroom. Are you going to get me a doctor now?"

"If you're still alive when I come out, I'll do that. Don't you yell out or I'll finish the job now."

Tom walked down a short distance and crossed the street just behind a wagon that lumbered by kicking up a lot of dust. There was a smell of fresh horse manure in the air.

Crossing the street without being seen, he entered the backdoor of the funeral parlor. He slowly pushed the door opened, but its creaking gave him away. There he was, the sheriff. When he drew his gun, he hesitated for a split second, just like Tom heard. Tom pulled his trigger and shot him in the right shoulder, knocking him back against the wall. With surprise Judd grunted and fired back, striking Tom in the leg.

"Really didn't think you could outdraw me, half-breed." He fired again, hitting Tom in the shoulder.

Tom shot again and hit Judd in his left hand. Another blast from Judd's gun and the bullet struck Tom in the lower left arm. Tom moved the doubled-barrel shotgun to his right hand and fired one barrel, hitting the sheriff just below the heart. His eyes had a glassed over stare in them as he fell backwards dead. The door opened and a woman stood there with a pistol aimed at Tom. She fired, hitting him in the lower belly. Tom fired the other barrel of his shotgun at her and she went flying backwards into the door and slid down to the floor. Blue smoke filled the room. When the shooting ceased, the townspeople were coming around to see who was still alive. Tom was in a bad way and was losing a lot of blood, but he was still conscious when the judge walked in.

"Did you get him, Sheriff?" He looked over to where Judd was lying and thought he was alive.

"No, he didn't get him, Judge." Potter jumped like he'd been shot.

"Just stand right where you are, Potter." The judge was looking into the barrel of a Peacemaker .45. "I might consider shootin' you before I die."

"I tried to get the sheriff to forget about you an' go about the business of protecting this town," the judge told him with fear in his eyes.

"You're a liar, an' you're behind the rustlin' also. If I live, you better be gone from this town. If not, you'll be dead."

Some men walked in with the doctor and he came right over to Tom, who was pointing his forty-five at him.

"Put it down, son. I'm here to help you." He turned to a couple of men standing there and said, "You boys pick him up gentle-like and get him up to my office. I'll see if I can do something for him."

In his office the doctor began to work on Tom, who had passed out.

"If I can save him it will be a miracle. He's been shot bad," he told his apprentice.

It had been a hot day and thunderheads were building up over the mountains. It wasn't long before it started raining, settling the dust in the streets and cooling things down. Doc Webber had done all he could do for him.

"We'll take him over to Martha's boardin' house. She said she'd look after him. There's nothing more I can do right now. He's been out for a spell."

Dr. Webber knocked and she came to the door and asked, "What can I do for you, Doc?"

"This young man has been shot up pretty bad an' will be needin' some care for a spell. Don't know if he'll make it or not."

"Well, you just bring him in, Doc, an' put him in the bedroom off to your right. That'll be right across the hall from my room. It will be a sight easier havin' him downstairs."

"You just let me know when you need me, Martha. Here's some medicine to give him. He is still in a coma. Don't know when he'll come out of it."

"Don't you fret yourself none, Doc. I'll take care of him an' with God's help we'll have him back good as new."

"I'll be obliged. I reckon he's a good man an' unjustly accused."

Doc Webber turned around opened the front door, walked out of Martha's and back to his office.

Judge Potter had called a meeting of the town council, including prosecuting attorney, Will Buttrow, and the defense lawyer, Vernal Stubbs.

"Will, something has to be done about Tom. He's killed the sheriff, another man an' that woman Judd hired out of Wyoming. Shot another man protecting McCrea an' he's up at the doc's, not expecting to live. On top of all this he has threatened to kill me if I don't leave town, an' accused me of rustlin' along with the sheriff."

"Judge, we're goin' to have a overall investigation into all this. Besides, Tom isn't goin' anywhere soon. He may not even live," replied Will.

"I'm in agreement with Will. If you are, you could go to prison and be disbarred," responded Vernal.

"If you don't mind, Judge Potter, we'd like you to leave while the town council an' ourselves come with a vote. We'll call you back in when we're through."

"Now that the judge is gone, Will, I vote we strip him of his powers until the investigation is over."

There were six councilmen and the two lawyers. The vote began. When the vote was in, six were for taking away his authority and two against.

One of the two that voted against spoke up. "We think he should have been kept on for the time being."

"We would be fools to keep him in power right now, Ken. We do need to vote on a temporary sheriff until we can have a general election by the citizens. My vote would be for William Tibbet who just came to town a short while back. He's a former lawman from California," remarked Will.

They all raised their hands in a yes vote for Tibbet for sheriff. They called Potter back in and told him of their decision.

"I don't agree with you of course. Who will judge any cases?" the judge asked.

"Will Buttrow will take care of that 'til this is settled."

"What's goin' to be done about a sheriff?"

"That has been taken care of, an' our advice to you, do not leave town," Vernal advised.

Tom came out of his coma. The first thing he wanted to do was get out of bed. He managed to throw his legs over the edge of the bed and tried getting up. It didn't work. He fell to the floor. Martha, hearing the noise, came running.

"What are you doing, Tom? For land's sake you're not able to get out of bed yet."

"I've got to get out of here and back to my Indian wife, an' besides I need to take care of that judge."

"The judge has been taken care. They didn't hang him, but he was found guilty of rustlin' among other things. He's been put away in the state prison for ten years."

"That's good news, but what about the sheriff?"

"You killed him in the shootout an' you were badly wounded. They hired an honest man for sheriff. Your friends from the Bar-0-1 came in to see you while you were unconscious. When you're well, they intend to take you back to the ranch."

"I can't stay there. I must get back to the Nez Perce in the Wallowas."

"You're not able to ride yet. The new sheriff received word that Pete has recovered and will be here before the snow flies," Martha told him.

Tom moved out to the ranch and was getting stronger everyday and planning to ride back to Mal-lit-tay-lay. In October Pete rode into the ranch.

"I'm glad to see you're alive, Tom. Didn't think I was goin' to make it myself for a spell."

"What are you goin' to do now, Pete?"

"Well for one thing, soon as you're able to ride, we'll go to the Wallowas but not before spring. There is too much snow now. Your wife is going to have a baby. She wanted to come with me, but I told her I would bring you back when the snow melted."

"I'm strong enough. Let's leave here now. She needs me."

"It's too late in the year to travel. Your woman will be fine with her people. We'll ride out in the spring."

It was November and snow was falling. Tom had improved considerably and was doing chores around the ranch to earn his keep. He'd been out feeding the bulls in the south pasture. He stepped into the bunkhouse, shook the snow off his coat, and the aroma of a pot of coffee on the pot-bellied stove filled the room. He walked over, poured a cup and remarked, "The snow's coming down right heavy. Getting' so deep I didn't think I was goin' to make it back. Sure be thankful when spring comes," he told Pete.

There was much work to be done every day, feeding and watering stock. Tom didn't think the time would ever get here when the snow would be gone. He was wondering how Mal-lit-tay-lay was. Did she miss him? Those thoughts entered his head. It had been a long, cold winter. In February, a warm Chinook wind blew down through the valley, melting the snow. Tom watched every day to see if any bare ground was showing. The month of March it began to rain and more snow melted.

"Let's leave now, Pete."

"No, we will wait two more weeks. April will be a good time," he replied.

Pete was right. Wasn't long before the wildflowers were popping through the skiffs of snow. Spring had arrived. Tom and Pete saddled their horses and rode north to the Wallowas and Mal-lit-tay-lay.